T0065631

A TIME FOR DEATH

Gaynor Cobb

authorHOUSE®

AuthorHouse™ UK
1663 Liberty Drive
Bloomington, IN 47403 USA
www.authorhouse.co.uk
Phone: 0800.197.4150

Published by AuthorHouse 08/31/2016

ISBN: 978-1-5246-6238-7 (sc)
ISBN: 978-1-5246-6239-4 (e)

DEDICATION

This book is dedicated to my family and friends who have gone before me into the light. May God bless them all.

INTRODUCTION

Have you ever wondered what happens at the moment of death? We all face it but no-one can really tell us about it. Throughout the ages, death has occurred in many different ways, sometimes a slow, expected demise but often quick and sudden. Of course, our view of death depends on our beliefs and whether we actually think that life after death is possible, or perhaps even probable!

These stories explore the circumstances leading up to and the precise moment when different characters leave their earthly lives. The stories do not end there and what happens after is imagined.

The first story begins in a hospital, with a modern day account of the death of an atheist, who believes strongly that death is a complete end with nothing beyond. After his death, the doctor and the chaplain reflect on their impression of the patient.

The stories that follow are set in different periods of history to consider the visit of the Grim Reaper. They are fictional and where they are based on events, some facts have been changed. For example, Leofwine probably died earlier in the battle than his brother Harold.

Like ripples in a pond, each life leaves something behind for history. The poems at the start and end of the book reflect the significance of life, death and history to the stories within.

TABLE OF CONTENTS

WE ARE THE PAST

The past is invisible.
Deep beneath the Earth, the changing strata of the rock,
betrays our origins,
How continents moved and climates changed.
As mankind grows, the past remains,
Hidden under stones we tread throughout life's years,
Accumulating layers of history on the bones of the forgotten.
Amid the detritus of the daily grind, lies treasure trove.
A Saxon bowl, a Viking buckle, a Roman sandal, long
discarded,
Buried underneath busy roads where traffic thunders
and pavements are pounded by the feet of centuries.

The past is seen.
Mighty castles standing strong, solid stone built to last.
Portcullis, drawbridge, moat, repelled invaders.
In towns and villages, amongst the cobbled streets,
half-timbered houses lean a twisted embrace across narrow
alleyways.
Iron horses, steam billowing out along great bridges and
tremendous viaducts,
celebrate our ingenious industrial heritage,
Schoolrooms holding blackboard, desk and cane,
nibs to dip in inkwells or chalk on slate.
Caps and pinafores, perhaps play-acting, re-create the days
gone by.

The past is felt.
Walking through the creaking lych-gate,
A winding path between moss-covered graves.
Within its silent stones the parish church,
echoes with wedding laughter, christening joy and funeral
tears.
A monument to milestones, three score years and ten.
Inscription lays bare the family life gone by,
Man, wife, soldier son and two dead infants remembered.
Real people stood around this grave and cried,
With arms outstretched in comfort, lilies of despair.

We are the past.
Childhood memories, stories Grandad told.
A changing world, inventions moving people on,
So easy just to blink and then forget.
What is life and who are we?
Pebbles tossed into the years, creating ripples.
Our bygone days are moments shared, friends' laughter,
family love.
The precious past is me and also you.
It is around us all, invisible, seen and felt.
Preserve it, for each one of us: Forever.

CROSSING OVER.

Gasping, Peter's breathing laboured and he felt his eyes, drugged and heavy, closing against the fading light of the room. *They've given up on me,* he thought and wondered if he'd given up on himself after all. He'd been fighting, determined to survive, every hour a victory: but why? He gasped again, knowing he was losing the battle. Why was life so dear to him when he couldn't think of anything to live for? His work perhaps? Even that had gone; the pain was too much. It was all too difficult, even breathing, just staying alive was a Herculean task.

So, this was where it ended: this hospital room: little of comfort. There were cards, curled and dusty, no messages of hope. What could they say, now they knew he was dying? Certainly not "Get Well." He was glad he couldn't see their faces now, the forlorn eyes: comfortless. He'd kept his sense of humour, just: cynical certainly. He would have laughed out loud (if he had been able) had he seen the sombre black figure passing by the door, pausing, hand hovering over the handle and then turning away with a shake of the head.

No, you're not going to save my soul. I'm not changing my mind, through some misplaced fear. This is it: the end. Peace at last. But not your peace. My peace; drifting into nothingness. Like putting out the lights and closing the door on life. All over now, no more pain. As you would say, alleluia to that. His chest tightened and the struggle increased with each laboured breath. *No more strength to fight,* he thought. *No-one here.* Why wait for them to watch him die? After all, they'd missed so much of his life.

Tears would fall, but bitter angry tears. Why them? Why should they have to suffer this? They'd think of his smoking and drinking: all the times he hadn't eaten properly and they'd blame him. Maybe not out loud in the open – they could never face truth – but in their hearts; yes, deep within their hearts, they'd blame him. What of him? Did he blame himself? Regrets? Surely it was too late now. Would things have been different, had he known?

The light faded, his breathing calmed as he sank into acceptance. His weak body cried out for release. Let go, it screamed silently at him, just let go. All his organs, veins, muscles, limbs, every cell in his sick being pleaded with him to call off the fight, to allow his humanity to slip into oblivion: for that was what it was. He'd spent his life proving it. Death was the end: nothingness. But what a great relief that would be: no more pain, no more worries. Just to end: bliss! So why was it so hard to let go?

The light dimmed. He was just awake. Peering into the darkness inside his head, he could see images forming. Now he really was losing it: seeing things. His mind was gone; death couldn't be far off now. How bright and clear the pictures were. A child walking in the woods with his parents; a young man climbing a mountain; people in the costumes of many countries. There was the girl: loving, laughing: friends sitting round a table: places of sun, snow and rain. He saw the images, fascinated, detached as though viewing a film; yet it was his life. Where were the struggles? The tears were not there. Was this life's last barb to make him want to cling to it? What a wonderful life in these pictures, but that was not the whole story.

As the colours died away, black and white faces drifted across his mind's screen. Who were they? They travelled swiftly beneath his sightless eyes, even as his breathing began to deepen and quicken. A force welled inside him, straining to get out. His brain pushed inside his head as though it would explode. Thought had gone. Just power surged; his life- force, ready to burst. It broke through and with a last, loud breath, his body was limp. The spark that was life, had gone. He had passed peacefully in the end (so they would say): alone.

Hurrying along the corridor, a busy nurse heard the unmistakeable sound of the monitor. When she opened the door, the line on the screen confirmed the urgency of the situation, so she called for a doctor to check the patient.

Despite its frequent visits, death still moved the practical Dr. Benson. The absence of a personality as a body lay lifeless could be felt, even among those whose suffering had meant that they were barely of this world near the end. Religious or not, there was a sense of reverence that hung around a death bed whether the passing had been peaceful or fought over by hospital staff. The doctor knew that nothing could be done in this case; it was all too late and anyway, the patient had suffered for so long that it was doubtful he would have welcomed a return to his ordeal. Dr Benson was still saddened by the demise of this man, who had born his pain with so much courage and often with a self-mocking wit which betrayed his sharp intellect. Peter's erudite exchanges would be missed, especially by the doctor, who realised how much he had enjoyed their conversations which were all too short amid the demands of his hospital work.

The chaplain, passing the room once more, noticed the stillness of the hospital staff. This time, he entered the room, knowing there would be no argument from the occupant of the bed.

"He's passed away then," the chaplain observed.

Dr. Benson turned sadly, "Yes, it's over for him now."

The chaplain readied himself for his own work. "A blessed release. He's gone to meet his maker."

The doctor gave a rueful smile. "If he meets his maker, it'll only be to have a debate and point out what's wrong with creation and the church in particular."

The chaplain nodded in agreement but glancing with uncertainty at the doctor, he looked down at the Bible in his hand.

"That may be so, but would you mind if I said a few words of prayer?"

Dr. Benson paused in thought, not quite sure what the correct response should be.

"He wouldn't thank you for it… but I suppose you can if you like."

The doctor stepped back and stood a little apart, respectfully, but without any desire to join in the prayers, which he knew would have angered his patient, surely causing death if he hadn't already died. He could see the irony of the situation. One way or another, he thought, they get you in the end.

Earlier…

As the last breath left his body, Peter felt a confused sense of release. The pain had gone. The tightness in his chest and the dull agony which permanently wrenched his stomach was no more. He was lightness itself. It was intoxicating, so different from the way he had suffered in torment, month after month. He realised with surprise that he was floating, with no ability to ground himself. He hovered in the corner of the room, looking down with the strangest sensation at the frail, grey body lying in the bed. Feeling detached, he could not find remorse within himself for the loss of life; the relief that he had left the broken shell behind him was so strong, almost euphoric. He started to move away from the vehicle his being no longer needed.

His shade though soundless, laughed out loud when the chaplain began to pray; he just couldn't help it. The bitter irony struck him, as words he had spoken seemed to drift around the room, caught up in a dream- like past. Perhaps he would need the chaplain's prayers after all. A wave of self pity washed over him, dragging him back down towards the hospital bed. He'd just died, but here he was, not knowing what would happen next. Expecting nothingness, real peace, an end to the ego that was Peter Tearson; yet the end had not come: an end of a sort, but what end, or what beginning? He didn't know because it had never occurred to him, even as the remotest possibility. He prided himself on his determination not to change his views, not to give in, even in the face of death itself. He had stood firm and looked death right in the eye. Death had won of course, as it always did. Now, he was going to find out the real truth. How the girl would have laughed at the absurdity of it all. No, that was unfair and blatantly untrue. She knew it would happen. How many times had she said so when they argued late into the night? Countless times, it was such a regular occurrence. He, (frustrated that she was so full of superstition, lacking a sense of scientific knowledge) explaining the rational view supported by his study of Astronomy and of course by Darwinian theory. She, (saddened by his lack of religion) stubbornly insisting that the complexity of the universe made it more likely that God did exist and that she knew deep inside that the soul survived death. But then, she was no scientist, the reverse: creative with imagination: too much imagination, he always thought. So, she was right; here he was, living proof, well, dying proof actually. He was still the same, cynical, self effacing being, no harp playing angel on a cloud, just himself. And where was everyone? He couldn't be the only person who had survived, especially here. How many people died each day in a large hospital? Should he try to look for them, the others, if there were any? He was starting to feel afraid. For the first time, he didn't know what to do. This wasn't supposed to happen. He was not prepared to be here. This was the unknown and he hated losing control. Panic started to move through him like a wave. He felt pulled down and saw a dark corner across the room. Shapes formed in the darkness. They became clearer and started beckoning to him.

"Join us," they called, "it's comforting in the dark. It hides the things we've done. You don't need God in the dark; he's not here."

He began to drift towards them and the pull grew stronger and stronger. His heart gave a flash of the girl again. This wouldn't be what she would do. The thought pulled him back and he stopped, uncertain. *But I'm not her; I rejected God. Why should he save me? It's too late for me. The darkness is my only hope, to hide from his sight for all eternity. I was wrong and now it's time to pay.* The shadows grinned their satisfied pleasure. They were sure he was on his way. One more to the dark side.

Suddenly he was overcome with all the love he had received during his life, along with the love he had given. This overwhelmed him and he knew it was all that really mattered: the essence of his being. For the first time, he was drawn towards a powerful light across the room. The desolate creatures of the shadows cried out to him, knowing their influence was draining away. Peter turned from the darkness with relief. As he moved away, he sensed his mother's love and desperately wanted to tell her that he had survived death. Her anguish and his despair dragged him back towards the lost souls and past them, he glimpsed the demons that knew they had lost their battle to claim his soul. For, having found love again, his logical mind reasoned with common sense that he had to push himself towards the light. It was more powerful than anything and was for him, the only way. He summoned all the soul -strength he could and turned away again. Peter felt the warmth of a spark of light within him which rejected the dark. Mind made up, sure of his path, he was accepted, healed, and forgiven in an instant. He moved along a tunnel of light, connecting with a part of himself long forgotten. He was complete and saturated with the wonder and innocence of youth.

Ahead, he saw the familiar figure of his grandmother, reaching out to him through the light. Flooded with warmth, he knew that he was going home, safe within the love of God; of whose existence he felt certain.

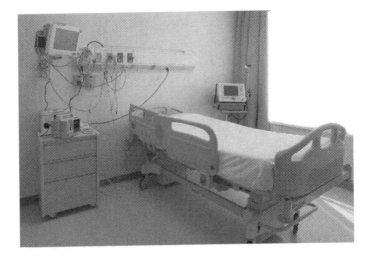

DEATHS ON THE NILE

The sun rose above the waters of the Nile. In the soft light and gentle heat of the morning, Nemraten, priestess of the Temple of Ra cleansed herself in the sacred river as she prepared for her daily duties. It was a special day. The Pharaoh had completed his reign on Earth and his body was to be laid to rest in the tomb that had been so carefully prepared for him. A multitude of treasures would be sealed within the tomb with his mummified body, helping his passage to the underworld where he would be received by the great god Osiris. There were many rites to perform to help the Pharaoh on his journey but first she hurried to complete her everyday tasks including the taking of food to the altar of the gods. She lit oil lamps and after placing them carefully in the required positions, turned her attention to the special blend of oils and spices that would burn throughout the internment ceremony later that morning.

Outside, as the sun rose higher in the sky, slaves laboured in the growing heat. Her spirits sank as she thought of their pain and of the frequent deaths of those who were worn out or moved too slowly to avoid the overseer's lash. Even within the temple, she could hear their cries amid the shouts and crack of the whips of their tormentors. She halted briefly to offer up a prayer to the god Ra to ease their suffering even though she knew they laboured for the good of Egypt and the Pharaoh. Hurrying to the robing room, she knew she had to make up time if she were to be ready to take her place with the welcoming party at the temple entrance.

When the sarcophagus was blessed and the gods implored to come to the Pharaoh's aid, they moved slowly to the tomb which had waited to receive its precious occupant. Deep inside the scorched earth, the last rituals of death were completed. Nemraten carried the sacred lamps and placed them around the sarcophagus. The flames flickered amongst the shadows, lighting the Pharaoh's way to the underworld. The light played against the walls, showing glimpses of the great leader's life. She stopped, held by the moment. This was the last service she could offer her Pharaoh and she was unable to stop a tear escaping from her eye. The slaves were ready to seal the tomb, so she hurried, not wanting to make their job even more difficult by the late hour. Even as she rushed away, she heard an echoing shout.

"What's going on?" the taskmaster called through the tunnel.

"Nothing! One of the idiots fell into the chasm. Don't worry, we've enough to finish the job."

"He's alive. We can reach him if we use this rope." A slave dared to suggest offering help.

"Quiet you! Save your strength to pull on the rope. You'll have to do his work as well as your own or you'll join him." A crack of the whip confirmed that the Egyptian meant what he said and the unfortunate slave was left to a slow death in the darkness of the tomb: forgotten. He was only a cog in a relentless wheel of toil and with many more like him, the wheel could roll on and on without mercy.

Weeks later, as she lay dying, Nemraten reflected on the events of that day. In her lucid moments, when the fever abated, her mind drifted back to the fading light inside the tomb. She saw herself watching the hieroglyphs and pictures of the great Pharaoh as they sprang to life in the glow of the oil lamps. Visualising the cold stone of the walls, she shivered, even though the fever raged. She had performed rituals for another soul, never considering that her time was near. The journey to the underworld approached and she who had prepared others, was herself unprepared. The nights and days merged into one. Drifting in and out of sleep, Nemraten thought about her life and of the world to come. In fitful dreams, she experienced the horrors of the journey to the underworld. Sometimes in fear, she failed to escape the serpent and was sent to eternal doom. When she succeeded in reaching Osiris, she watched the ceremony as her heart was weighed against a feather on the scales of Ma'at by Anubis. She awoke panic stricken, sure that her life had been found wanting.

On one such night, she felt a cooling cloth pressed gently against her forehead. A soft voice came through the darkness, as her weak body jolted with the terror of the nightmare. "Rest, Nemraten and may the god Ra grant you peace." Nemraten strained her unfocused eyes without recognition. "Who?" she managed to whisper.

"Only, Lefretis, your friend," replied the voice.

Nemraten tried to smile and pressed the fingers of the hand she found she was already holding. Remembering the dream, she returned to the question that plagued her feverish mind.

"Will I pass the test?"

Lefretis could sense agitation as she watched a cloud pass over Nemraten's eyes, almost igniting them into life, though sparked by fear.

"Test? There is nothing to worry about, just rest now."

She dipped the cloth into cooling water and moistened the parched lips of her patient. Speaking more easily, Nemraten explained, "My heart, weighed against the feather. Will I pass the test? I will won't I … but then…I saw Ammit the Devourer and she opened wide her jaws."

Realisation dawned for Lefretis. Why had she been so slow? Her friend's attention had turned to death and perhaps more importantly… to judgement. Again, Lefretis soothed, "Of course you will pass the test. You have a virtuous heart and you have served the great god Ra with so much devotion. Rest easy. Ammit's jaws will open in dismay. There will be nothing for her." Lefretis could feel her friend relax. A sigh escaped her lips and she murmured, "Thank you. It will be soon."

"No! If you can only rest, you will begin to feel better again." Even as the words passed her lips, Lefretis knew that she was offering false hope. Nemraten however, was clear despite her fever.

"It will. The darkness comes. Wish me luck."

"You do not need it. The gods will welcome you." Lefretis found it hard to cool the fever. She could feel her own heart beating faster as she struggled to help her friend. She saw Nemraten's hand feel around her neck, thin and wasted by disease.

"My amulet?" Nemraten spluttered the word, but Lefretis knew the significance of the sacred amulet of Ra.

Her eyes searched the room and finding it, she placed it in the dying woman's hands. Almost as though she was satisfied that all was well, Nemraten took a laboured breath of relief and was still.

"It is over." Lefretis closed the staring eyes as her tears fell silently onto the amulet making it shine in the oil-lamp's glow. The shadows on the walls did not reveal the ghostly presence of those who had waited for the passing of Nemraten. As the news spread, souls were drawn to the chamber in the hope of adding to their number.

"Come sister, join us among the living as we watch the glories of Egypt unfold."

Nemraten, remained transfixed by the scene below as Lefretis tended her body, whilst crying soundless tears. She was overcome by the desire to comfort her friend; to reassure her that there was no need to mourn. After all, here she was, Nemraten, still in the room as before, but no longer in pain and discomfort. Death had claimed her, but it was a strange relief, almost exhilarating that she no longer suffered the agony of illness.

The ghosts grew impatient. They had no compassion for the living (or the dead).

"Do not linger by your broken body. It is nothing now. Leave the living to mourn.

Come with us and see what you can do, freed from the shackles of a mortal frame. It is just skin and bones. Even the blood to spill is gone. Turn away from the corpse and live with the dead!"

Their hollow laughter seemed to echo, so that Nemraten was forced to notice them but she found it hard to take her eyes away from Lefretis, who kept a vigil near the body.

"Nemraten, Nemraten, Nemraten."

The whispers grew louder and they crowded around her, trying to block out the sight of her friend.

"Who are you? Are you from the underworld?" Nemraten's fears came flooding back. They laughed again.

"No, we are not from the underworld. We are here and we have no desire to join Osiris, or Anubis. We do not need them. They cannot touch us."

The shade of Nemraten shuddered but did not know why.

"I have to start my journey into the underworld, to take the test. My heart must be weighed against a feather."

The ghosts stretched out their hands, trying to grasp her shoulders and pull her towards them. She flinched away, although it was an illusion. They had no power to force her with physical strength. Their attack was of the mind and it continued.

"Forget the perils of travel into the land of Osiris. Leave empty the scales of Ma'at and defy Anubis. We have defeated them because we will not go." Nemraten recoiled.

"What are you afraid of? Why do you stay here, bound to the earth?"

Encouraged, they approached, summoning all their persuasion.

"It is our choice. We are happy here. You will be safe with us."

Nemraten wanted desperately to avoid the perils of the underworld but she felt uneasy. She had prepared all her life for this moment. To pass into eternity was her purpose from birth. Her everyday work within the temple was devoted to this future. She knew that she must follow the sacred path whatever happened. There was no easy way out. She had to make the journey, to take the test. As this certainty overwhelmed her she became aware of a bright light in the corner of the room. The ghosts wailed in desperation, knowing that she was moving away from whatever power they possessed. They shouted,

"No, No! You must come with us. We need you. You are ours, our Nemraten. You can't go."

Nemraten did not need to answer them. They had lost. As soon as she had made up her mind, she moved quickly towards the light which appeared to draw her in more strongly, increasing her determination to leave the ghosts behind. With one last look around the chamber, Nemraten sent a wave of love to Lefretis, who prayed silently by the lifeless body. The ghosts were starting to drift away, melting into the shadows, powerless to change her decision. Realising their dilemma, she could not help the pity and compassion that streamed out of her soul towards them. They were consumed by fear and so unable to move on as she knew they should. Her fears existed but she began to realise that they were groundless. This was how it was meant to be. She had already passed a test and would face the future unafraid. She turned towards the light with certainty and looked into it with contentment.

Within the brightness, she could see two figures, becoming clearer as she moved into the golden haze. She recognised her parents, smiling as they reached out to her. Whatever the journey, she knew that there was really nothing to fear. Having made the right choice, she was surrounded with love. Their guidance and support would help her on the journey. She had no doubts about the outcome, only sorrow for those left behind. She moved towards eternity with satisfaction, knowing without a shadow of doubt that the scales would balance.

BEHOLD THE MAN

He ran through the dusty streets of Jerusalem panting, heart pounding and feet thumping the hot stones as fast as his broken sandals would allow. Behind him, the Roman army, (well, a few of them) advancing with their quiet efficiency, organised and deadly. They were fit and their sandals were sturdy. They would catch him up easily, unless he was lucky or managed to outsmart them. His eyes flashed around in desperation, looking for a way out; anything to give him half a chance.

Dodging into a dark alleyway might work but a dead end could prove fatal (literally!). He recognised a way through, a short-cut to the temple. They wouldn't arrest him in the Jews' holy place, especially during Passover; that could start a rebellion. All in all, the Romans just wanted an easy life; an occupation that ran smoothly, to send taxes back to the Emperor in Rome.

The crowds increased as he neared the temple. He raced on, trying to avoid the swarming bodies. It was harder to keep up speed. He was flagging and people were all around him. He had managed to throw off the soldiers but not for long he felt sure. He had to push his way, weaving and dodging in the crush. They would have no problem with the crowds, who would part in fear to let them through, just as Moses had parted the Red Sea when pursued by the Egyptians. He dared not look back but he was sure they were close behind. Another corner and he would be at the temple. Could he keep going? He felt ready to collapse. One last spurt of energy was all he needed; it would be enough. He pushed his body on into the crowd and increased speed in a final desperate effort. Throwing himself headlong, he collided with some baskets of olives, sending the slippery fruit flying in all directions. The olive seller let out a stream of curses, realising the enormity of his loss and turned to see the advancing soldiers.

"Here, he's over here! Look, he's ruined my olives! Get him! A man should be able to make an honest living. A thief no doubt. Thief! Thief!"

The fugitive had no time to help gather the fruit or listen to the tirade. He ran on, leaving behind a scene of oily confusion. Nearby beggars and others in the crowd, gathered up the olives, returning some uneaten to the baskets but at the same time, a profusion of pips landed in the dust. The soldiers appeared, drawn to the commotion and the olive seller's protestations but showed no sympathy. They tried to continue their pursuit and their shouts carried across the crowded street, so that Thaddeus knew his luck had not deserted him. The soldiers were clearly angry that the slippery ground and hungry crowd were in their path, along with a nuisance of an olive seller who was unable to get out of their way fast enough.

Thaddeus slipped into the temple courtyard and propelled himself towards a dark corner, where he propped himself up, panting against a wall to catch his breath. After a few minutes he was recovered enough to take in his surroundings. The usual hustle and bustle, busier he thought because of the Passover festival. Plenty of money-changers and traders selling birds and animals. They were robbers just like him; what was the difference? He stood reflecting on this pearl of wisdom, when a ripple of excitement ran through the crowded courtyard.

"He's coming. He's on his way here"

"No, he's here. Just wait, he's coming in. Make way!"

Shouts rang out, echoing round the ancient stones. Who were they talking about?

In just a few minutes, it was clear. The teacher from Nazareth, who had ridden into the city that day to loud acclaim, was at the temple. People had followed after, laying palm leaves before him and shouting praise to the 'King of the Jews.' That explained the streets, even more crowded than usual and the excited throngs around him now. The temple courtyard, already teaming with creatures of all kinds, some of them human, was full to bursting. It was a perfect place to hide while everything calmed down outside. Thaddeus enjoyed people watching, (that was what made him such a good thief) so he was fascinated by what happened next.

The crowd parted to allow the teacher to get to the traders. He looked at some birds flapping around a cage and seemed to cast his eyes around the whole scene. With a sudden movement, he grabbed a table covered with temple money and hurled it to the floor, taking several other tables with it and scattering animals, birds and money around the courtyard.

"This is my Father's house but you have turned it into a den of thieves," he shouted, storming through the crowd and turning over more tables. The traders were furious. They hardly knew whether to attack him, or try to recover their money and animals. Birds squawked, feathers flying in all directions, making Thaddeus dive out of the way.

The teacher had moved on into the temple with people still following to hear him speak. Thaddeus observed the Chief Priests huddled together and knew by their glowering faces that the teacher had enemies. It was not only robbers who had to watch their backs in Jerusalem. He felt that it was time to risk the street again. With luck, the soldiers would be gone and he would be able to slip away without any fuss.

Outside, the sky was sunset- red and the crowds were thinning. He could hear murmurs of disbelief at the events inside the temple. The teacher was certainly the talk of the city. Melting into the crowd, he kept his ears open to hear more and his eyes open for any easy money. It was there, a money-bag, hanging temptingly from a rich man's belt. How could he resist? He deserved it after such a day. With one quick slight of hand it was gone but only as the man reached for his shekels and cried out in despair.

"My money! It's gone! You...it's you. You've taken it. Thief, thief! Thief, thief! Stop him! He's taken my money!"

Thaddeus didn't look back, he fled towards the end of the street, where his sandal finally snapped and he tripped into the outstretched arms of a Roman soldier. The soldier gripped him firmly and he felt the tip of a spear pushed into his chest. He groaned as his skin was pierced but kept quite still, knowing that any movement would cost him his life. The Roman laughed,

"We lost you before, but the gods must be smiling on me today. Here you are my thieving friend and this time, we have you. I do not think you will steal again."

The soldiers tied his hands and led him away. Thaddeus knew he had been stupid; he should have disappeared without trying his luck again; he had escaped once, it should have been enough.

Days later, Thaddeus waited in line to begin the long walk towards Calvary, the hill of execution. His spirit was broken and his bruised body covered in dried blood. His mind swam, dizzy with pain, so that he hadn't the strength to fear death. It would put an end to his misery and that could only be good. He could not think about the pain of the cross, the most immediate thing was to find the strength to carry the heavy wood across the city.

By the time they reached Golgotha (Place of the Skull), Thaddeus was dazed with agony. He hoped for a quick end to his wretched life but knew that the cross was a slow way to die, chosen by the Romans for those who opposed their rule and meant to discourage dissent.

Thaddeus was tied onto the cross while large nails were driven into his hands and feet. It took three soldiers to move the cross into position on the hillside where he would meet his end. Gradually, through the pain, Thaddeus became aware of those around him. There were two other crosses together on the hill. The man nearest to Thaddeus, who was in the centre of the three, was being singled out for especially harsh treatment. The soldiers were jeering at him. His body looked broken already, bruised and bloody with the scourge of the whip. A sign had been nailed onto his cross which said, "This is Jesus, the King of the Jews." Thaddeus remembered the man from the temple. He had been impressed by the way he had tackled the thieves there and he had provided a good diversion. People had been talking about him all week, excited by the things he had said and done. They even said he had healed the sick. Now where were his supporters? It seemed that the crowds had turned against him. Truly, these people were easily swayed. The soldiers threw dice to decide who would have his clothes. They hurled abuse at him, as did many of the passers by.

"You're the one who claimed to be able to tear down the temple and build it again in three days. Save yourself and come down from the cross."

Even the criminal on the other side joined in. "Save yourself and us too, if you are the Messiah!"

Thaddeus surprised himself when he shouted out in reply. "Aren't you afraid of God's anger? We're all being punished in the same way but we deserve it; we're guilty. This man didn't do anything wrong."

The other criminal fell silent, probably in too much pain to argue. Thaddeus turned his head towards Jesus. "Will you remember me when you take power?"

"I promise you that today you will be with me in Paradise."

Thaddeus felt comforted by the reply. He had heard Jesus asking forgiveness for those who killed him, saying that they didn't know what they were doing. There seemed no doubt that the man was special. No ordinary criminal would behave like this. The drugged wine was affecting Thaddeus, dulling some of the pain and making his mind confused and yet he knew that Jesus had refused to drink it.

By the middle of the day, the sky darkened, even though the sun should have been shining. The soldiers around the cross started to become nervous and the crowd stopped shouting insults. God is angry, thought Thaddeus. Now, they're not so sure of themselves. Some of the people started to drift away, realising that they did not want to be associated with the death; the atmosphere was heavy and oppressive. Whispers appeared to echo among the onlookers who remained. "What if he is the Messiah? What will God do to us?"

The echoing whispers seemed to magnify the agony of the cross and Thaddeus felt that he was drifting painfully into the darkness that surrounded him. He couldn't think but didn't want to. He closed his eyes but the pain was worse.

The whispers stopped. An eerie stillness held the pain at bursting point and a voice cried out, "My God, my God, why have you deserted me?" Another shout could be heard and then silence. Thaddeus forced his eyes open but knew that Jesus had died. A nearby Roman officer shook his head. "This man really was the Son of God," he said.

The darkness started to clear, though Thaddeus did not want the light. Even dead, Jesus was still causing a commotion. After a while, murmurs could be heard again.

"The curtain in the temple tore in two from top to bottom. It must have happened at the same time he died. The ground shook with tremors. We could feel the anger of the Lord. What will we do now?"

"Paradise! I'll be in Paradise," Thaddeus murmured aloud.

"Sooner than you think," came a rough voice, as a soldier thumped a sword hilt onto Thaddeus's knees, breaking them to collapse his lungs. Thaddeus shouted in strangled agony, his breath squeezed from his body. The end had come quickly so that the Jewish Passover would not be tarnished by the dead and dying.

Darkness wrapped itself around Thaddeus, his soul slipping into eternity. He could see his broken body on the cross but appeared to look on with detachment, no longer connected to it by pain and the emotion of life. He really didn't care much about life; it had never been much good. Somehow, he couldn't get it right; he did not fit in. Well, it didn't matter now. It was over; what happened next?

He could feel the oppression of the place and the events which had occurred there. The air was heavy; even the dead were pulled down by its sorrow. The trauma of execution could not be pushed away easily, it lingered like a dense fog around his shade. The black, cold gripped his soul like a vice, forcing waves of emotion which would have fallen as tears, had he been alive. Was he destined to haunt this place of death, adding to its desolation? Thaddeus could not see relief in death if that was so. He thought about Jesus and his promise. He was the Son of God, of that Thaddeus was certain and yet he had died in pain, like Thaddeus. Why? Thaddeus could not understand. Maybe one day he would know the answer. Jesus had died with quiet dignity and a calm courage. Anyone could see that he was special. Why had he been condemned? He was innocent and had given the people hope and healing. Why was good so often destroyed?

Strangely, the thoughts of Jesus had comforted him, so that he was drifting away from the darkness. A haze, purple-pink collected around him, bringing some heat to remove the chill. It became deeper in colour and merged with deepest blue. Through the colour came the brightest light he had ever seen. He was fascinated by the strength of it as it flooded through his being with great warmth. In the centre of the light, Thaddeus could see Jesus, surrounded by winged beings which could only be angels. The man who had died on a cross next to him, reached out towards Thaddeus with smiling love.

"Come, my friend, this is Paradise indeed. You have suffered with me and have found belief. Your sins are forgiven."

LEOFWINE, BELOVED BROTHER

Leofwine had stood shoulder to shoulder with his brothers ever since Harold had been proclaimed king and for longer, if he thought about it. Edward the Confessor had made Harold his heir and he was accepted as so by Saxon Britain. He would make a good king in Leofwine's opinion and that was not just brotherly bias.

However, there was a problem, in the person of the 'bastard Duke William', who felt that the throne should be his because of an earlier promise by Edward and a forced pledge of subservience from Harold when he had been held captive in France. Once free, Harold's oath should have been meaningless and it seemed clear to Leofwine that Edward's will should be the deciding factor. This indeed was the Saxon view and they were prepared to defend it. News had come that Duke William was gathering an army to invade Britain. A Norman should not rule this wild, untamed land, perhaps in absent control; Leofwine would sacrifice his life before he would allow this. William would have to wait for the wind to be right before he could sail and that could mean a significant delay but they meant to be ready for him. Would the French nobles be any match for tough Saxon fighters armed with two-handed battle-axes? Leofwine trusted that they would not!

Harold had assembled his army with the aid of his brothers Leofwine and Gyrd. The Earls helped him to gather local leaders who led the 'fyrd', forming the warriors and peasants into wedge -shaped battalions with the best soldiers at the point. Even though the peasants were almost useless, fighting with whatever they could lay their hands on, the sheer numbers of them threatened the enemy and could weigh the balance in a close fight. In any case, the lords were bound to fulfil their obligation and bring the men of their household to battle. It was a truth that all Saxons had to defend their king.

When news had reached Gyrd and Leofwine that Harold Hadrada had invaded in the North supported by their brother Tostig, they wanted to ignore it. Leofwine had sat with his brothers staring into the dying embers of the camp fire, and the more he pondered, the more certain he became.

"We can only deal with one threat at a time and the greatest is from the bastard Duke, of that I am sure."

Gyrd nodded in agreement.

"If we stay here, we can meet his army as they step from their ships. Norman blood will soak our Saxon beaches before they gain a foothold on our land."

The plan was clear and surely invincible, but Harold could not agree.

"I have sworn to protect the people. I must march North to repel the invaders. Thus, I will show them the way of a true king."

Leofwine's eyes blazed.

"If you do not defeat the bastard, your kingship will be short -lived, my brother."

Gyrd weighed his words carefully.

"I am of the same opinion as my brother. If we defeat the Normans, we can march North in triumph, knowing London is safe."

Despite their fervent arguments, Harold would not be persuaded.

"William is not here now; Hadrada is. We go North for battle and hope the Normans are delayed until our return. The seas could be rough and the winds against them. Ready the men, we leave at daybreak."

The King had spoken and so it was. The brothers set aside their doubts and prepared for the long march North.

They met the enemy at Stamford Bridge in Yorkshire and put them to flight, leaving Hardrada and Tostig both dead. Despite this success, their own numerous loses in the course of the battle made it feel more like a defeat, knowing as they did that they would soon be fighting again.

News reached them that Duke William had landed at Pevensey, even though he had been driven back into the sea by the men of Romney in Kent when he had tried to land there. Nevertheless, he was organising his army. He had time to be ready to face them and was all the stronger for this. Leofwine knew that with the battering they had taken and a long march back to Sussex, they would need to gather reinforcements before they returned for the fight.

Once again, Harold was stubborn.

"We will march at sunrise," he insisted.

"But, Sire, given time, Gyrd and I can bring together men to form a fighting force. We must replace those who have been felled."

"There's no time Leofwine. We must go. I mean to destroy Duke William. Every day, he is growing more settled, more powerful. I cannot delay. Saxons fight hard to the death. We will defeat him and certainly, he will not expect us so soon. The power of surprise will be on our side."

Leofwine sighed, knowing that argument was pointless, no matter how reasoned.

"Of course, we are with you my brother, till death parts us."

They clasped hands and drank a toast with heavy mead. Leofwine was partial to the honeyed drink made by monks. He hoped that his head would be clear when the time to march arrived with the morning light.

The men were battle-weary and struggled at times over the rough terrain. The victory had kept their spirits high but Leofwine knew that even strong Saxons needed to recover. He could feel it in his own bones; the damp autumn nights seeped into his battle aches, despite some sharp, fresh days of exhilarating (but forced) optimism. Indeed, they sang when they could and kept their blades sharpened and readied.

They arrived outside Hastings on a misty morning and Gyrd took a party to check the lie of the land. Much of the area was wooded but a clearing was found near the Norman position and the Saxons set up their army on Caldbec Hill, along the ridge. It was a sound military position and with sharp, wooden stakes forming a protective fence along a defensive ditch, even Leofwine was well pleased. He spoke to the housecarls positioned in front of his brother, although he had little need of reassurance that they would shield Harold until the last one fell. Hopefully, the battle would be long won before then.

By the next morning (14th October 1066), both Saxons and Normans were ready. They were so different in composition and approach; the combat would be challenging. No-one could tell who the victors would be. Leofwine prayed that God would be on their side.

Harold instructed the Saxons to hold their position. When under attack, they fought on foot, running forward with cries of "ut, ut" (out, out) and imploring the strength of the Almighty with shouts of "Godemite." The Normans used horses to attack, trying to break through the Saxon ranks. Many of the horses were struck down, so that even Duke William had to use three different mounts and rumours grew that he had met his end. In desperation, he threw off his helmet and toured the battlefield, showing all that he still lived and was unharmed. His brother Oddo, violent and ungodly, did the same, rallying the tired Normans to face the foe.

As wave upon wave of Normans rode into their defensive line, Leofwine shouted in despair.

"Hold, hold! In the name of the Holy Cross!"

The lines had broken but upon his words, the retreating Saxons turned and stormed towards the Normans with shouts and screams. Leofwine led the army back into shape, taking Norman lives as he rode fiercely towards the enemy.

It was early afternoon and the battle had raged for hours, with skirmishes on all sides. The Saxons held their line and in so doing, gave the Normans little chance of success. They were exhausted, but sensed victory. The peasants of the fyrd had fought bravely. Seeing their chance, they forced through the flank of Bretons, charging towards the Frenchmen. As soon as Leofwine saw them hurtling down in hot pursuit, he knew that the Normans would be able to penetrate the Saxon lines at last. Arrows fell like rain, fired by skilled Norman archers and their nobles rode up to the ridge with Saxons hewn, like dying English oaks. The Saxon army started to fragment, its organisation shattered by the weakness of inexperience and enthusiasm. Leofwine looked round the battlefield for Harold. His brother was protected by the loyal housecarls but the only hope was to get him away. Perhaps another army, on another day could still take William and his French invaders.

Leofwine decided to fight his way through to Harold and try to persuade him to retreat.

He wondered if he was alone in thinking that the battle could not be won, yet he could sense desperation in the fierce fighting of the men around him.

Leofwine's blade flashed and sliced through the Normans until he neared Harold's position. He tried to call out to his brother, but the noise of battle prevented him. He moved nearer, just as a barrage of Norman arrows hit the wall of Saxons. He saw Harold fall, which made him lunge through the enemy with even more determination to reach the wounded king. The Normans had broken through, taking away the Saxon advantage at the top of the slope. Panic spread all around, as the Saxons realised they were exposed to the ferocity of the Normans, who were among them and fighting with agility and skill. Leofwine however wielded his trusty axe: a powerful friend. He fought on, so that Norman bodies collected at his feet.

Another avalanche of arrows came out of the clouds, as Leofwine neared the spot where his brother lay. He carried on, desperate to reach Harold.

When the arrow hit, he felt the sharp pain but the exhilaration of battle deadened his senses and his reactions. He staggered sideways and was felled by the blow of a sword. Leofwine lay among the dying, knowing that the Saxons had failed. He would have given his life for his brother and died, content that Saxon strength had prevailed and they had won the day. Now, his life's blood ebbed away and he knew that his sacrifice was in vain. William had won. Leofwine's despair mingled with excruciating pain and he gasped his last breaths.

He was high above the battlefield, floating in a black mist of misery. He felt lighter than he had during battle and no longer in pain, but his heart was heavy with sorrow. Leofwine sensed the anguish of the dead and wounded, who cried out with silent screams. The darkness pulled at him and he could see mountains of broken bodies on the hill, sunken into the red earth.

Through his confusion, Leofwine realised that he had not survived the battle. His body lay among the Saxon dead, along with those of his brothers, Harold and Gyrd. His thoughts turned to them and he was aware of their presence close by, although he could not see them. The battlefield was thick with the ghosts of the dead, stumbling and drifting around; human debris unable to change the outcome. Many of the living Saxons had fled, but those who had stayed to fight perished in the fray, fighting for a lost cause. Without their king and his brothers, they had no order and discipline to their battle and they were easily picked off by the Normans, who quickly smelt victory.

Leofwine's soul was full of sorrow as he joined with Harold. He had been unable to protect his brother and preserve the Saxon crown. The darkness crushed his spirit but the love for his brothers transcended despair, breaking through the drifting black clouds to show a spark of light.

Above the dark, suspended gloom, Leofwine noticed a midnight -blue sky with sunset-orange light on a far horizon. It was there, but appeared unreachable and he remained held by the torment of anger and frustrated loss that had swept through his earthly body as it fought, reaching his soul. With the dawn of stark reality, Leofwine realised that so much of his existence had been spent wielding an axe in battle, struggling against human life in a fight for domination. What did it matter now? With dark shame, he wished that he had spent more time in prayer; had he missed the chance to save his soul? Would he be consigned to the fires of Hell? If he had given alms to the poor, or the beggars at the castle gate, he could have moved towards the light with some hope of salvation. He had fought, yelling shouts of "God Almighty" and "The Holy Cross." Yet, to kill in the name of Christ seemed wrong, now that he was forced to reflect on it. These thoughts swept through his shade, battering its substance as though he battled a different foe: his conscience.

Leofwine looked around him at the dead and knew that many would remain earthbound. He could feel their pain and bewilderment; their guilt consumed them and they did not know how to free themselves. They fought with hate and anger, sure that God was on their side; but whose side was God on?

The Normans, though victors, had also suffered loses. Their dead were drawn to the celebrating knights but were unseen. Theirs was a hollow victory; to them no spoils of war as they had been promised, or feast of triumph. They would not return to France or settle in the conquered acres of a foreign land. Leofwine could not hate them; they had fought with valour and had done their duty to their lord and to their God. He knew it was the same duty: the Father, Son and Holy Spirit. It was not just Harold and Gyrd who were his brothers, it was all humanity.

The cold, darkness of the battlefield faded with its ghosts and Leofwine drifted towards healing blue light, as warmth spread through his being. Harold and Gyrd were at his side and he knew they too had journeyed through the pain of self evaluation. Life was a struggle with no room for blame or self pity. All that was left at the end of the battle of existence was trust in God's mercy: to pray for forgiveness and to forgive others.

"Forgive us our trespasses as we forgive those who trespass against us."

Leofwine, beloved brother could finally hope for Heaven.

FATAL KNIGHTS

Matthew rushed towards the altar, crossing himself. "Forgive me, Lord," he whispered as he wondered why he was always in a hurry. Monks were supposed to be serene, other worldly, carrying out their duties with measured movement rather than the quick panic and lack of organisation that was his nature. He had so much to do before Vespers and he really had meant to be early.

In the quiet moments, as he lit candles in preparation, he offered up a silent prayer for his abbot, Thomas, returned from France after his exile. Although he prayed with every fibre of his being, he feared that little could be done to repair the broken relationship between Thomas Becket and Henry II and therefore between Church and State. Becket still refused to repeal his excommunication of the Bishops of London and Salisbury following their support of the king. Certainly, the truce between prelate and monarch was uneasy.

As the light died, Matthew was joined by his brother monks and the cathedral was filled with singing to God's glory on the fifth day after Christmas. He had always loved this special time of year when days were shorter and candles lit the ancient stones. Shadows played on the walls in the flickering light, as inside the frosty air seemed banished by the warmth of worship. Peace and friendship appeared stronger after the festivities and all seemed to be in good voice. It was this upon which he concentrated, trying to keep out thoughts of trouble and raging kings.

After all, what could possibly go wrong in this most blessed season when all energies were turned towards the praise of Christ the Lord?

Thomas Becket had been working quietly, attending to the many day to day tasks that had accumulated since he had been away in France. Time rushed past with so much to do but he realised that, as darkness fell, he was missing Vespers. Setting aside his papers, he hurried towards the cathedral. Before he reached the door, he heard the clatter of horses' hooves on the cobbles. Shouts rang out and now listening intently, he could hear the unmistakable sound of swords being drawn. Half turning, he recognised his name being called. Certainly, these were no friendly visitors whom he should bid welcome. The strange feeling in the pit of his stomach told him that as he had feared, Henry had not ceded the power of the crown to God. With quiet determination, he continued and entered the holy building. The shouts were louder now and it was clear that he was being pursued. The monks had become aware of the commotion and had halted the service. Matthew and many of the monks ran to meet Thomas at the door. As the last chants of Vespers died away, they were replaced by angry threats from unwelcome strangers.

Thomas entered the magnificent building, determined to retain a semblance of calm. Once the archbishop was inside, Matthew pushed against the heavy doors, trying with all his might to force it shut. Several of the monks had the same idea. They must protect their abbot against these madmen.

Thomas' voice rang out clearly amid the disturbance.

"It is not proper that a house of prayer, a church of Christ, be made a fortress."

He insisted that the service should continue, speaking so calmly despite his despair.

"We will triumph over the enemy through suffering rather than fighting, and we come to suffer, not to resist."

Matthew was shaken. What could Abbot Thomas mean? To give in, to be a martyr?

So like our Lord, he thought. *Yet, why be a martyr for the sake of Henry?* Despite his misgivings, Matthew moved away from the doors and followed Thomas as he walked slowly towards the altar. He could see the archbishop's lips moving in silent prayer and added his own desperate appeal to God for help in this hour of need. Matthew and his fellow monks surrounded Thomas so that he could not be seen.

The threat had not retreated; it hid in the shadows. The flickering light threw grotesque images onto the walls; four knights with swords drawn stalked the sacred stones.

A disembodied voice came from the darkness.

"Where is Thomas Becket, traitor of the king and kingdom?"

Matthew shuddered. For a brief moment, the words hung in the silence. The candlelight caught a flash of blade, as they turned, brandishing their swords which were raised in anger. It seemed unreal to Matthew in the place of prayer.

Another voice, "Where is the archbishop?"

Before the monks could respond, Thomas spoke, his voice strong and without the slightest tremor,

"The righteous will be like a bold lion, free from fear." He turned from the altar and met the eyes of the fearsome knights.

"Here I am, not a traitor of the king, but a priest; why do you seek me? Here I am, ready to suffer in the name of He who redeemed me with his blood; God forbid that I should flee on account of your swords or that I should depart from righteousness."

Matthew heard the knights demand that Thomas should restore to communion and office the suspended bishops but Thomas stood firm and refused to give in to their threats.

"No penance has been made, so I will not absolve them," he replied calmly.

Matthew knew that the knights would not leave. They had come for one purpose and would not back away now. He thought he could detect a satisfied triumph in the voice of the knight who cried out,

"You will now die and will suffer what you have earned."

As they spoke, they were closer to Thomas and attempted to drag him outside but could not move him from the pillar near the altar. Thomas had decided where he would meet his fate. In this, at least, he would be triumphant.

"I am prepared to die for my Lord, so that in my blood, the church will attain liberty and peace, but in the name of Almighty God, I forbid that you hurt my men, either cleric or layman in any way."

Although Thomas tried to reason with Rainaldus, one of the knights, who he sensed had been led by the others, his calm reasoning was met with even greater force and anger as the knight realised there was no going back. He swayed, raising his sword in an almost drunken rage. Matthew tried to place himself between the sword and the archbishop and to push the knights away. Perhaps they were drunk and would sink into stupor and shame. He prayed as he used all the strength he possessed, but he was no match for the knights. He fell bleeding, trying to cover and protect the archbishop, but was thrown aside as the knights determined to reach their prey. Thomas bowed his head, as if in prayer and did not utter a cry as he sank to his knees under the blows. His final words were spoken in a low voice.

"For the name of Jesus and the protection of the church, I am ready to embrace death."

Matthew gasped his last, thinking only of the archbishop. He would have been happy to have given his own life to protect Thomas Becket, but he had failed dismally.

The four knights turned away from the altar, leaving the monks crowding round the blood soaked stones. As the sound of their footsteps were heard leaving the scene, they did not look back to check on their handiwork; they knew that their mission was accomplished. No doubt they would be honoured by the king. They had followed his command and had indeed rid him of the turbulent priest.

Matthew watched the knights as they replaced their bloody swords in their scabbards and walked back through the darkness. He could see their faces clearly, even in the candlelight. Through the triumph, he even thought he could see fear creeping its way into their souls. It passed like a shadow across their eyes, although they fought hard not to let it in. The deed was done, this was no time for regrets, but… it was a rash act, to kill a man of God. When they died, they would rot in Hell, if such a place existed. Rainaldus, if drunk indeed, had sobered rapidly. Hanging back, he hesitated and casting down his head, he went to cross himself then thought better of it. He pushed open the heavy door and strode out into the night. A snow storm had started, so that an eerie silence descended upon the cathedral close. No words were spoken as they rode away, the necessary bravado would come… later.

The knights gone, Matthew turned his attention to the scene at the altar, where the grieving monks, bewildered and distraught, tried to come to terms with the death of their leader. Firstly, they performed the act which came most naturally to them; with bowed heads they knelt and prayed, as they had never prayed before. Matthew joined their prayers and then noticed that they had placed richly embroidered cloths over the blood spattered floor. He felt as though he was in a dream and then he realised. Why had he not seen before? The archbishop was there, standing, bathed in light, watching as he was, transfixed by the sorrowful scene. *Why doesn't he tell them he's alive, just as I am?* Matthew thought. As he wondered about this, he was there with Thomas Becket, who stretched out his hands and made the sign of the cross to him. Matthew's mind was flooded with words from the archbishop.

"My son, you were courageous in trying to save me. I am so sad that you had to pay the price when it was for me to face Henry's henchmen. I had turned from a friend of this world to serve my master in the next and now I am happy to be going home to him."

Matthew did not understand. "My Lord Archbishop, we are alive. I don't know how, but we are here. You must tell them not to grieve. The blows did not kill us and I am unhurt."

Becket was nearer, shaking his head.

"Sadly, Matthew that is not the case. We are certainly dead. Our bodies lie beneath those covers which hide the bloody deed of Henry's misguided knights. I know my friend and fear he will not welcome the news as they believe he will. I cannot think he meant for this to happen. He is prone to rages, but they are often swiftly denied."

Realisation began to dawn and Matthew had to accept that the archbishop was right. The more he thought about his situation, it made sense that he had indeed survived death, as the church had preached. But where was Heaven? Where were the angels and Christ himself?

"Why are we not in Heaven, my lord? We are still bound to our earthly lives."

The archbishop was unperturbed.

"Look around you my son. Try to see past the scene of grief. Look above the high altar, at the beautiful stained glass window. So often have I gazed in wonder upon it, but never have I seen it as it is today."

Matthew forced himself to turn from the tragic scene of carnage and followed his abbot's instructions. As he did so, he felt his whole being flood with warmth. A golden light flowed from the window, drawing him towards it with a steady force.

The archbishop held out his hands.

"Come my son, we will enter Heaven together. I can already hear the voices of angels singing."

Matthew looked back to see the solemn chanting monks and wondered if it was their voices that could be heard by Abbot Thomas. When he turned once again to the light however, he could see a host of angels and knew that he could indeed hear their song. He was there beside the martyred archbishop and they were on their way to Paradise to be with their Lord Jesus Christ.

DEAD OF NIGHT

Jacob Deakins peered through the fog, trying to discern the shape of a small boat and straining to hear the faint splash of oars, which would signal the long awaited arrival. He shivered as he turned to the man alongside him.

"Had a feeling about tonight. Don't know why I left my bed."

"You'll know soon enough, Jacob. It'll be a good night's work. We couldn't have better weather for our purpose."

Jacob had to agree.

"You're right Will. Can't fathom why I'm such a misery. Just an old feeling in me bones." He laughed but it was nervous, forced laughter, making his companion shudder, as if someone had walked over his grave.

There was no more time to dwell on Jacob's dread fears, as the quiet sound of oars against water drifted towards them on the sea breeze. Jacob recovered himself and called out,

"Come on lads, set to."

Dark shapes moved through the foggy night going about their business with measured efficiency. The men waded through the shallow waters to pull the boat up onto the beach. Boots sank into the muddied sand but if they noticed, they did not react, used as they were to this night work. The boat beached; they moved barrels carefully. Jacob barked out instructions, experienced as he was in directing operations.

"Look lively, boys. You'll be tucked up like babes within the hour."

The men passed the barrels along, taking care not to let them fall into the waves which lapped the shore. They were stowed inside two old carts and covered over. Some small brandy barrels and pouches of 'baccy' were carried by the men on horseback. No-one intended to put all the 'eggs' in one basket!

The boat was pushed out to sea and soon disappeared into the fog once more, so that again, only the faint splash of oars could be heard on the still night air.

Although the thick fog seemed to be lifting (at least inland), mist floated sporadically over the marsh, as night gave way to early morning.

It won't be long now, thought Jacob, as he mounted his horse which was heavy laden with brandy and tobacco.

"Ready then?" He shot a glance at Will, who shook the reins of the horse, so that the cart set off with as fast a pace as possible. They made reasonable progress towards their destination and stopped a little way off, to await the signal. Peering through the mist, a deserted church tower rose up from the marshland, a ruin, gaunt and skeletal against the sky. A light could be seen, though faintly and in intermittent flashes. Jacob gave a low sigh of relief. All was well. They could proceed and the business could be concluded.

Will drove the cart up to the lych-gate, while Jacob tied his horse nearby. They unloaded the barrels and two chests of tobacco, leaving them behind a mildewed tombstone. They pushed open the heavy church door. Inside, all was quiet. Strangely, there was no wizened old sexton rushing to meet them as usual and Jacob's eyes searched through the gloomy interior in an attempt to find a sign of life. The signal had been unmistakeable, unless they were both marsh-mad!

"Where is he?" Will's whisper was hoarse with fear as the reality of their situation set in. The answer was not long in coming.

"Halt! Put down your weapons in the name of the King." The voice seemed to come from the direction of the bell tower.

Jacob had no intention of giving up his pistol. Instead, he pointed it in the direction of the voice and fired.

"Get down," he shouted at Will, before throwing himself headlong into a box pew.

"I'm not dancing on the end of a rope. I'm getting out of here", Will called out and ran for the door. Two shots rang out and Jacob heard a groan, followed by a thud.

"Will…Will…?" Jacob whispered as loudly as he dared, trying not to give his own position away. Of course, there was no answer. He lay flat, knowing that he was alone facing the excise and wondering how many there were. It would be a miracle if he got out alive but he knew that Will was right. It was better to go down fighting than to face the hangman's noose; of that he was certain.

He heard heavy footfalls echoing through the church.

"Well, have it your own way. We're coming to get you, ready or not!"

A hollow laugh announced the deadly game and Jacob knew that they would find him if he stayed put. His only hope was to risk running for it, just as Will had and in reality he knew that his chances weren't much better. He moved to the edge of the pew and crouched in the darkness, hardly daring to breathe. His heart thumped so hard against his chest that he felt sure they would hear it. *At the count of three*, he thought, *then I'll go for it.*

One, two, three...

Jacob crawled out, straightened up and ran for the door, keeping his head down as much as he could. Only seconds passed, before the church echoed to sound of gunfire once again.

The pain came, sharp in his back and he gasped as he knew that he had been hit. Nevertheless, he carried on running and found himself outside the church facing row upon row of overgrown gravestones. He had no recollection of even opening the church door, although it was obvious that he had. He really was losing his mind!

What about Will? he thought, feeling guilty. *What if he is still alive?* He told himself that he should go back for the friend who had been in so many scrapes with him, but he knew that he wouldn't; it would be suicide. After all, *Will must be dead, mustn't he?* It was no matter, Jacob knew he'd been lucky to get out and that luck was unlikely to hold, especially if he was carrying his wounded friend. Best to make it home as quick as he could and lie low until the fuss died down. Maybe he could even take a small barrel of brandy, or a bit of baccy. What was he thinking? Barely escaping with his life and still planning to get away with some of the stash. Well, he was a true gentleman of the night. *Marsh folk are tough, there is no doubt of it!* He laughed to himself as he picked out the tombstone which hid the contraband.

Yes, he reassured himself, *Will must be dead.* The only thing to do was to get away as quickly as possible. He remembered with dismay that he had felt pain himself, another reason for quitting the scene. He felt fine now and there didn't seem to be any blood, at least none that he could see. He wondered why the excisemen had not pursued him. It was not like them to give up the hunt for their prey. His musings were interrupted by the sound of the heavy oak door swinging open with a bang. Out ran armed excisemen. Jacob ducked behind a nearby gravestone, hoping they would not find him, or the hidden barrels.

"Right lads. Search every blade of grass until you find it. There's a full tankard at 'The Ship' for the man who spots it first."

No mention was made of Jacob, but he knew that it would be hard to stay hidden in such a thorough search. He would have to find the right time to run for it again, even if it meant leaving the horse behind and heading across the marsh on foot. However, he decided to try the horse first if he could get to the lych-gate. Reluctantly, he accepted that he would have to leave the barrels behind and be satisfied with getting away with his life.

Some of the excisemen went round the back of the church but there were several still too close to him for an easy get away. He would have to hope for luck. It had held so far. Just a bit longer, not too much to ask. If he had been a religious man, he might have prayed. But then, how would God feel about his occupation? True enough, there were a fair few black frocks glad to take the brandy and baccy but not many who would take the risks. He wondered what had happened to the old sexton. He'd no doubt met his maker that night. *Had they made him dig his own grave; he had dug so many others over the years? He wouldn't even have his drink of brandy and a smoke of his pipe.* Jacob's thoughts spun round and round as time hung in the balance. The foggy night had given way to a morning marsh mist and that usually came with a chill that went straight through to the bones.

A shout went up from behind the old Martin vault.

"I can see them. They've put them over there. It's that stone covered in ivy."

The excisemen ran towards the voice even though the mist swirled around the churchyard.

Now's the time, thought Jacob. *Go Now*!

He ran for the lych-gate without looking back but this time there were no shots behind him. Hardly believing his luck, he decided to try for his horse. He waited in the darkness of the lych-gate, glad to have survived so far, deciding that the marsh mist was a wonderful thing indeed. Slowly, he reached out to take the horse's bridle, wondering if he would be able to ride away from the church safe into the marsh. The horse shied and reared up, its hooves bearing down on him.

"Now, now. Thunder, it's me, your old friend."

He couldn't bring the animal under control, it kicked out and he had no idea what to do next.

"That horse is spooked," a voice cried out and he was aware of a hand taking the reins away from him.

"There boy, there. Calm yourself. There's nothing to be afeared of; though your master won't be coming back for you."

The exciseman patted and stroked the horse and did manage to settle it down. Jacob stared open mouthed at the man, who seemed to look right through him. The horse, nostrils still flared, shifted nervously despite the man's calming influence.

"He can't see you because you're dead Jacob." The unmistakeable voice of Will made Jacob turn round. Sure enough, standing just behind the exciseman was the strong figure of Will, unscathed, even though his blood-soaked body had laid on the church floor.

Will continued, "You're in there, or what's left of you, same as me. We never made it. Never likely to were we, when you think about it?

Jacob had to agree. How could he have been so blind? Yes, it was obvious. He never stood a chance. There was no luck, not this time; it had run out. Once the realisation had been made, Jacob tried to come to terms with his situation. He had never thought about being dead and now felt relief that Will was in the same condition. He had no idea what happened to dead people.

"What now?" he asked, turning away from his horse which calmed in an instant.

"That depends. It's up to you. Do you want to face St. Peter, or stay with them?" Will gestured towards the edge of the graveyard, where Jacob became aware of a number of shadowy figures coming closer and closer.

"Who are they?" he asked Will, who seemed to have all the answers.

"Oh, they're the earthbound. Those who have died but have not moved on; sometimes because (like you), they don't realise that they're dead; or they're afraid to go to Heaven because they've done something wrong and they think they'll be sent straight to Hell. I think some are smugglers, like us."

Jacob thought about all the things he had done and knew that he wasn't at all sure he was ready for Heaven. Who was ready for Heaven anyway? He couldn't think of more than a couple of people who were really good. Most of the folks he knew had a good few skeletons in the closet.

"What do you think? We've done plenty wrong. Are we like them? They don't look too happy to me. I think they're in their own Hell and I don't want to join them, though I'm not sure what choice we really have."

Will nodded with understanding as he watched the phantoms advance. He shook his head with a shudder, as if to shake them away and looked beyond the lych-gate at the brightest light he had ever seen.

"No, Jacob. It's our choice. I'm going to the light. It feels warm, like home. I want to get away from this cold place full of death and fear. What do you think ? Are you with me? We've always taken chances; this is one last chance but I don't think it'll be a bad one."

Jacob also looked away from the shadows of the graveyard into the light and knew that his old friend was right. They'd had many night time adventures on the Marsh and this was the start of another one.

He was decided.

"Aye Will, I've never been much of a betting man, but if I were, I'd wager that yonder light is the way to go. Come on, it's been some night and it's not over yet. We didn't give the excise the slip but we can outrun those shades, I'll be bound."

Always game to take a risk, their minds focused on the way ahead and they found themselves drawn towards the powerful brightness which eventually blocked out everything else. The marsh gloom and the ghostly churchyard were gone as they moved with certainty into the light of a new beginning.

SKY WOLF

Sky Wolf crouched at the edge of the forest, gazing through the trees with intensity, scouring the undergrowth for signs of movement. It was dusk, the best time for hunting, and his sharp hearing picked up the sound of rustling leaves along with the swishing of disturbed branches. He was an expert tracker, taught by the best: Red Cloud. His mentor had indeed watched the pupil grow and learn with an eager determination until pupil outperformed master and it was time for Sky Wolf to hunt alone.

Now, Sky Wolf enjoyed the quiet of the trees, but he missed his teacher and friend, wishing that Red Cloud had not passed beyond the horizon to be with the Great Spirit. Indeed, he had lived to a good age, but would have seen many more summers if it had not been for the white settlers. Their hands had not killed Red Cloud in the honour of battle, but worse, the disease brought by the strangers had felled him. His body had tried to fight the unknown enemy until it had no strength left. Sinking into inevitable death, he had felt humiliated, beaten by a strange foe, believing that he had deserted his people at their time of greatest need. Many had suffered a similar fate, defeated by the creeping menace which had proved stronger than wolves or bears.

Sky Wolf stopped to look up as he tracked his prey. He asked the spirit of Red Cloud to be with him as he moved silently through the forest. Red Cloud, smiling, watched over the young brave, knowing that he had no need of help to achieve success. Sky Wolf heard the graceful deer before they knew of his arrival. His arrows flew, certain and sure to their marks and his collection of fur and feathers became greater as darkness fell.

When all the light had faded away, Sky Wolf returned to the clearing to set up his camp for the night. He was content out among the stars. At peace, he was one with nature. Sky Wolf loved this time alone. He stared deep into the night sky, counting the stars and feeling close to his ancestors. He could sense the closeness of Red Cloud, who he knew would approve of his day's hunting. Collecting stones, he prepared a fire for the night, to cook some food, keep warm and to ward off intruders. As he piled brushwood in the centre of the stones, his sharp eyes caught a quick movement on the periphery of his vision. At once he was alert, the fire not ready, he needed protection. A flash, a howl, a reaching out of the hand, grasp, throw, watch... With a thud, the animal hit the ground, eyes staring, blood oozing from the place where the tomahawk had struck. Brother wolf had landed at the feet of his namesake, peaceful in death despite his ferocity in life. Sky Wolf moved the animal gently, sad that he had been forced to kill this brave creature but aware that his own life had been saved. Indeed the wolf would not have shown him mercy, that much he realised. So, when the fire was lit, he took the skin and the proud head to adorn his battle dress. He had not sought this, but he was Wolf; it was his right.

After eating, he sat reflecting on the day as he stared into the flames. He offered up thanks to the Great Spirit, to his ancestors and to Red Cloud. He honoured the brave animals who had made the sacrifice to sustain his life and the needs of his tribe. They were his friends, giving, along with their skins and meat, attributes that would serve him well. The deer showed him how to run through the trees with agility and a lightness of foot. The wolf had guile and fierce courage; it knew the pack loyalty that he felt towards his tribe. He had learned from them as he had taken lessons from all creatures; Red Cloud had seen to that. Understanding the place of man within nature perfectly, when Sky Wolf finally settled down to sleep, he was at peace, sensing the beating heart of the world around him.

Dawn came with the red sun rising above the forest. Trees and grass glistened with dew and the early morning light crept through the misty air. Sky Wolf woke to see an intricate spider's web hanging from a branch just above him, reaching to an adjoining tree like an ethereal archway. He marvelled at the skill of the spider as he trapped his prey, much as Sky Wolf had done the day before.

Despite the glories of nature, the young brave knew he must not linger in the clearing. It would be a long journey back to his tribe and like the creatures around him, Sky Wolf hurried into the tasks of the day. Everything had its job within the cycle of life and his was to make speed to deliver the gains of his day's hunting.

He was soon riding back, sure of a happy welcome and keen to return, well laden, to his loved ones. His horse travelled lightly across the ground, despite the extra weight. Anxious to make haste, he turned from his usual path. Using a more direct route, he covered the distance quickly and could see by the position of the sun in the sky, that he would soon reach his destination.

Leaving the dense forest behind, he could see that the open land was scarred by fences. *Ugly things* he thought, as he jumped first one and then another, clearing the tops easily in an attempt to get back to his usual route. *More fences!* He groaned in dismay. Why had he decided to go back a different way? This was a change, but certainly not a good one. He did not want to have to make camp for another night, to fend off other animals from the spoils of his kill. Why did white men try to control nature in this way? Didn't they know that the land could not be taken? It could not belong to anyone, but must be honoured, cared for and owned by all. Everything; person, plant, animal, rock was part of the same creation. The Great Spirit meant for man to understand his connection to the world around him. The thoughts brought on a bad mood which he tried to shake off. He tried to forget the settlers and to concentrate on crossing the obstacles, sure that once away and riding free again, his good humour would be restored.

He turned the horse to clear the next fence, then another. Just two more and he would be riding clear once again.

Out of the corner of his eye, he saw the flash, the spark and the noise which brought his horse to its knees with a sickening thud. The horse's head lolled to one side and its body shuddered with the impact of a bullet. Sky Wolf heard shouting but he didn't wait to understand what was said. Like lightning he found his bow, took aim and fired a quickly placed arrow at the owner of the smoking gun. He reached for his tomahawk and advanced upon the enemy.

The arrow struck the settler on the shoulder disabling his aim. He clutched his wound in panic as he watched the young Indian brave stride towards him brandishing a fearsome weapon. The tomahawk flew swiftly hitting its mark. The man cried out in pain, blood gushing from his chest and he fell to the ground. Sky Wolf uttered a sigh of relief, knowing that he had defeated his attacker but the rifle fired again as the man's body fell on top of it.

It's over, thought Sky Wolf, approaching the settler who lay face down on his gun. People nearby had obviously heard the gunfire and were rushing to see what had happened. Sky Wolf turned in fear, as two men armed with rifles appeared. His tomahawk rested in the body on the ground and he knew that there would be no time to remove it. He felt for his arrows and his bow but they were not on his shoulder. Anyway, his quick mind calculated that even if he felled one of the white-men, the other would certainly finish him. Despite this, he was determined to go down fighting. He fought off his own fear; he would not disgrace his people. He remembered the knife in his pocket, so at least he would be able to leap at them with a fierce war-cry. He reached for his knife and launched himself towards the approaching settlers.

"Hokahey!" he shouted, as he leapt into battle.

He landed on the ground without any contact and there was no knife in his hand. The men unhurt, ran past him and rolled the white-man over, removing the tomahawk.

"It's no use, he's dead," said one.

The other searched the trees carefully, rifle poised to shoot, but soon lowered it.

"Well, at least he got the redskin before he went. I reckon it was just one of 'em. Either that, or they high-tailed it outa here."

Sky Wolf stared down at the body, annoyed at not getting his tomahawk, but turned, trying to understand what the white-man was talking about. Had he left a trail of blood? He couldn't feel any injuries. The dreadful realisation washed over his being like a shock wave. At the man's feet, lay another body covered in blood with lifeless, staring eyes and a hand that gripped a bow. Now, Sky Wolf knew why the men did not notice him.

He was dead! Why had he not realised? His first feelings were of anger with himself and also with the paleface who had killed him. He had been so close to home and now he would not be able to take the food and furs to his tribe. They would have been of great use. His anger gave way to a deep sadness which intensified as he thought of the softness of Naomi, his squaw. Now they would not lie together on the warm furs he had taken.

Red Cloud had taught him more than hunting. His mentor had instructed him in deeper matters ; he had learned other lessons. Now, he had to turn his thoughts away from the concerns of life. He knew that he needed to concentrate on the hereafter but this was hard to do. His life and that of his people was close to death; they understood that everything had a time. He knew that he must find the way to go so that he could be with his ancestors and move towards the Great Spirit.

As he drifted with his thoughts, he was aware of a shadow passing over him. The settler, although on the ground was not going to give up in death. He ran at Sky Wolf, but passed through him harmlessly. His frustrated rage dragged him towards his neighbours and he tried to attract their attention without success. Sky Wolf felt sorry for the settler, who lacked his understanding of death. The young brave knew that the anger he had felt himself was pointless; it could not change what had happened. The main thing now was to find the way forward, to move toward the Great Spirit.

"We cannot hurt each other now, my pale- faced friend. We must move on to be with our ancestors. Come, we can both find a way." He approached the settler but was brushed aside.

The settler turned in anger, his face a picture of desperate disbelief. A shiver seemed to run through his whole body and he froze with shock. Reluctantly he forced himself to examine the scene. He could hardly bear to look at the body he had so recently vacated, but when he did, he realised that it was a lifeless shell. It lay in a pool of blood on top of the rifle. Nearby, lay the Indian brave who did not seem so fierce in death as in life.

"All right, we're dead. So what happens now, seeing as you seem to know all about it?"

This was almost a challenge and yet in truth, Sky Wolf did not know what happened next. So often, he had searched the stars or the fire flames for an answer to that most important question. He knelt with his head close to the earth and spoke to the Great Spirit from the depth of his soul. The answer came almost at once, flooding through his whole being.

"Let go," it said. "Release your soul from the ties of life and embrace the hereafter."

The truth resounded within him and as he accepted this knowledge with belief, he felt as though the weight of life had indeed been taken from him. He was ready to join with his Indian ancestors and with his mentor, Red Cloud. Above, the sky was replaced by golden light, so bright that it blocked out everything else. It was nothing and everything. Sky Wolf felt that he could soar above the earth and fulfil the true meaning of his name. Truly, he would be one with nature: the real nature of Spirit.

He reached out his hand to the settler.

"Come, my brother. We must go together into the light. Where we are going there are no enemies, only friends."

Only a Minute

Jeremiah Wilson pulled back the drapes and looked out into the night. The sky was clear, allowing the stars to shine with a rare brightness and the moon hung full like a grinning face. He shivered, although it was hardly cold; it was a nervous tremor, which would have translated into petrified fear had he thought about the night ahead.

"You're not going tonight, are you Jem? Leave it to the men; they're fools enough to take on the 'lobster backs' on their own, without dragging boys into the quarrel."

His mother put a steaming pie on the table and proceeded to cut a good slice, which she set aside for him.

"I'm eighteen Ma, old enough to fight for my rights, like the next man. We can't pay the taxes and we should have a say in it, at least."

She would not be persuaded and he knew it was a waste of time trying, but he had spent days trying to make her understand.

"I still say it's sending boys to do a man's job and a foolish one at that. Anyway, you'd better come and eat. If you insist on dying, you'd better do it with a full belly.

Noah was out shooting rabbits last night and they've made a right tasty pie."

Jem was not sure that he could eat a mouthful but Ma's rabbit pies were the best for miles around and he knew it made sense to eat something. It was going to be a long night and there was no telling when he would get the chance to eat again. Besides, maybe food would take the sick feeling away (either that, or make him throw up, which would finish his chances of going completely!) His brother was already tucking into the pie and it was disappearing fast.

"If you don't make your mind up, little brother, there'll be none left for you anyway." Noah said with a laugh.

Jem sat down at the table and had to admit that the pie was as good as ever. He was glad that he had decided to eat.

Noah took his side, which was a rare event.

"You've got to let him go, Ma. Folks round here are going to talk for years to come about tonight. Jem deserves to be part of it; we all do."

Ruth Wilson levelled a steady gaze at her eldest son. He was tall and strong like his father, calm and reliable, full of that common sense that was so uncommon! She knew he was right; she could not stop Jem. She could not have people calling him a coward when it was all over.

"Well, you look out for him, Noah Wilson. You look out for your brother and bring him back to me."

She dissolved into the tears that had been threatening all day and sank into a chair by the hearth. Jem went over to her and put a comforting arm around her shoulder.

"I'll be all right Ma, just you see. I'll make you proud of me. I promise."

"And, I will take care of him, Ma. I swear to you on Pa's Bible."

Noah took the heavy family Bible down from the shelf above the chair where his father had liked to sit.

Through her sobs, his mother nodded. "There's no need to swear on the Bible, Son. I know you'll look after Jem."

Noah returned the Bible to its place of honour, finished eating and went over to the window. He was looking for the pre-arranged sign that would tell him to assemble on the Green. They were ready and waiting, muskets polished and primed for the task. He was anxious to get started; he hated hanging around; it was better to get on with it. He peered out into the darkness but could not see any sign of the signal he was waiting for.

The hands on the clock moved round and Ruth put aside her darning reluctantly. She told herself that no news, meant that the night could pass without incident after all. Folks were often all talk; there was nothing like a good rumour to get everyone riled up good and proper! She climbed the stairs to bed but didn't try to persuade her sons to give up their watch. She knew that would be a waste of breath. They were too like their father : born stubborn.

Noah and Jem sat by the dying embers of the fire, saying little. Every now and then, one of them would go over to the window and stare out towards the church, hoping to catch sight of some movement in the tower. Jem had even fallen asleep for an hour and Noah couldn't think of a reason to wake him as nothing was happening and it was likely that if anything did, he would be glad of the rest.

When Jem woke, it was with a start. The situation came flooding back to him in a flash.

"Maybe we're getting jumpy for no reason. Just 'cos Adams and Hancock are laying low here, it don't mean the Brits are gonna come after 'em and risk a fight." Jem still sounded nervous.

Noah turned back from the window.

"I know what I said afore, but you don' have to fight. There's no folks as would hold it agin yer."

Jem was quiet for a moment, as though he was turning the idea over in his mind but then he shook his head.

"I sure ain't gonna back out now. Reckon I'll see it through. Besides, someone's gotta look after you an' stop yer shooting all those lobster backs with that shiny new musket there."

Noah laughed.

"Well I sure feel a whole lot better knowing you'll be looking out for me! Still you could be right. There's been no signal and it'll be morning afore long."

The laughter made Noah feel better and he decided that the chances of trouble had virtually disappeared. Jem was right to say that the whole town had been jumpy, since Samuel Adams and John Hancock had decided to stay there. He thought about his comfortable bed upstairs and was just about to announce his intention of turning in, when the church bell sounded, shattering the stillness of the night. He roused himself quickly and rushed to the window. He could not make out anything clearly but he knew it didn't matter. He was a minuteman and had to be ready in a minute. Jem was quickly at his side and they made it to the door without noticing their mother or hearing her call out to them from the top of the stairs.

Outside, figures moved almost silently towards the Green, stopping about halfway between the Meeting House and Buckman's Tavern. Paul Revere and other riders had ridden from Boston to warn the townsfolk that the 'Regulars' were coming and the alarm had been sounded. The commander, Captain John Parker organised the men. Some were prepared with weapons, but others had joined the ranks and needed to be armed. Despite the warning, there was no word of the Regulars along the road, but this time, Jem was sure that they would come. Noah had given him their father's old musket, so he was ready, unlike some he knew as he looked around. He noticed Captain Parker receiving a message and then saw him call up William Diman, the drummer to beat arms.

The drum beat echoed around the Green, as the light struggled to signal a new day through the fog.

The Captain spoke to the men.

"Don't fire unless fired upon. But if they want a war let it begin here."

Noah gave Jem a reassuring pat on the back.

"Good luck, little brother. I know you'll do Pa proud with that musket."

Jem nodded, but didn't know what to say. Before he had time to think, the Regulars could be seen coming through the fog towards the Green. Strangely, the sick feeling that Jem had had all night seemed to have gone. He strained his eyes to see the soldiers and to weigh up the threat. A voice could be heard but he couldn't see whose it was and then he noticed the British Officer at the front of he column.

"Lay down your arms, you damned rebels, or you are all dead men... Fire!"

Shots rang out but no-one seemed to be hit. Jem decided that it had only been a warning. For an eternity, the minutemen held their position and tension rippled through the dawn. However, faced with the experienced regulars, the raw recruits sensed that they were unlikely to defeat their enemy. It was to be hoped that Adams and Hancock were safely away. The lines of minutemen had certainly created a diversion that would hold Pitcairn's men up and help the men of Concord to conceal the arsenal they had been gathering.

John Parker feared for the safety of the young men he commanded; most of them had little experience of battle. They were all keen, patriotic youngsters, who were surely prepared to die for their principles and the rights of their country but there would be other battles they would have a chance of winning. Sometimes you had to know when to fight, to pick your battle.

With these thoughts in mind, he ordered the company to disperse and told every man to take care of himself.

Jem heard the Captain's words but could hardly believe it. He had spent so long waiting to fight, waiting to make his family proud, to prove that he had grown up, that he could be as good as Noah. He looked around for his brother but could not see him among the confused minutemen, who after spoiling for a fight were beginning to run. The Regulars held their line, used to taking orders and a cautious approach.

Jem was still looking for Noah, when it happened: a single shot rang out across the Green. He couldn't tell where it came from, or even which side was responsible for

'the shot heard round the world', but within seconds the noise and smoke of musket fire battered the very air around him. Dan Peters from the forge slumped to the ground inches away and Jem reached out to help him but saw that it was too late. Blood gushed from a deep wound in his chest and his lifeless eyes stared up without response, even when Jem tripped over his arms which had twisted awkwardly under his vast frame as he fell.

Muskets were firing on all sides now and Jem was conscious of his father's precious musket, still clasped firmly in his hand. He hardly knew which way to point it in the confusion but his instinct was to return fire rather than run from the fray. He got to his feet and took aim, pointing the musket into the smoke. He remembered all the times he had practised, waiting for this opportunity. Now that the time had come, he didn't feel the thrill he had thought, just blind terror and a numb response to the chaos around him.

A voice called through the smoke."Jem! Jem! Get out of there!"

Jem looked round but couldn't see where Noah was, even though his voice was unmistakeable. The words however registered in his addled mind; he had to get away. He tried to see a path through the foggy smoke around him but hardly knew which direction to go.

When it hit him, the pain struck, mingled with the noise, smoke and fog, clogging his brain, so that he staggered on through the bodies of the living and the dead, hardly realising what had happened. Shock and adrenalin combined, enabling him to move away from the fight.

"Jem, hold on to me." Noah's voice was there again, although Jem still couldn't see him. He felt a strong arm around his shoulder and for a second the pain appeared to lift a little.

Noah steered Jem into the woods, knowing it was not safe to return home, at least not for a while. He laid his brother down on the bracken under a tree and looked to see where he had been shot. The bloody clothes around his chest revealed the place where the musket ball had entered Jem's body and Noah knew that it needed to be taken out if his brother was to have a chance of survival. He took out his pocket knife, wondering if it was sharp enough and if he was sufficiently calm to extract the shot. He knew the answer. Jem would only have a chance if they returned home, so that he could be properly tended. They would have to risk being caught. He could not even afford to wait for nightfall; it would be too late. Jem needed help as quickly as possible.

When he thought about it in later years, Noah could never work out how he managed to get Jem to the house. Ruth always said he had the stubbornness and determination of his father and that was true. He took advantage of the general confusion and made it to the back door with Jem propped up against the old oak in the garden.

Ruth hurried to answer the furtive knock. She had been waiting anxiously for news ever since she had watched them leave before dawn. When she saw Noah, she almost cried with relief but bit back her tears.

"Ma, I've got Jem outside; he's hurt bad."

Noah didn't stop for an answer; he rushed back to the tree where he had left Jem. His heart was pounding as he checked for a pulse before hauling Jem towards the open door. Ruth gasped when she saw her youngest son covered in blood, his white face showing how near he was to death.

"The Regulars?" Noah looked questioningly at his mother.

"I don't know. There's no more shooting now but I reckon they'll be searchin'." Noah had to agree.

"I know it's not safe Ma but it's Jem's only chance. We got to get the shot out of him."

Ruth didn't need convincing.

"If we can get him upstairs, it'll buy us some time if the Regulars come calling."

With difficulty, they managed to carry Jem to his bed. Ruth boiled some water and they cleaned the wound. Noah found the sharpest knife in the house and sharpened it again.. He put it in the flames of the fire which Ruth had kept alight from the night before and hoped that it would be safe to use. He went upstairs and motioned to his mother to hold Jem down. Noah hoped that his hands would not shake as he took a deep breath, uttered a fervent prayer and dug the blade into his brother's chest as carefully as he could. Jem had lost consciousness but the renewed pain of the knife brought him back with a feeble cry. He groaned and mumbled incoherently, as they fought to stem the blood and cool his fever.

Inside his head, Jem was still fighting his first battle. He stumbled through it in confusion, firing at Redcoats and watching them fall onto the grass. On falling, they could no longer be seen because they seemed to merge into a sea of red. He could not tell how many he had killed because of this but his musket kept firing, over and over again, without the need to re-load. Noah drifted into the melee but Jem was angry with him. Noah seemed to want him to leave the battlefield but he was having so much success and so he fought against his brother's attempts to pull him away. Why did Noah always think he was right? Just because he was the eldest, he thought he always knew best. This time, Jem was going to be the hero. Ma (and Pa in Heaven), and Noah (if he would only admit it) were going to be so proud of him.

When he felt the knife, he cried out with the fierce pain, jolted back to reality momentarily. His eyes opened in disbelief. Where was he and what had happened to him? He became aware of the bed and shadowy figures leaning over him, who appeared to be Noah and Ma. Was he at home and in his own bed? How could that be possible? Maybe it was the battle that had been unreal, but then why did he hurt so much and feel so sick with the pain? If this was a dream, it was a nightmare and he couldn't wait to wake up with everything back to normal.

"Try to sleep now, Jem. You're safe now. Get some rest."

Ruth tried to soothe the pain, but there was little she could do.

"He's losing too much blood, Ma. He needs the doc. I'll go and get Doc Mulhearn; he'll know what to do."

Noah rushed to the door and down the stairs, without thinking of his own safety. Ruth couldn't stop him but she hardly knew what to think. One son was dying in front of her and the other had run out into the path of danger. She hadn't time to think about it; there was so much to do, just trying to staunch the free flow of blood from Jem's wounds. Jem was drifting in and out of consciousness but he felt her soothing hands, work- roughened but gentle with love.

Ruth was pulled away from the bedside with a loud banging on the door below. Her whole body shuddered with fear as she realised that the Regulars must be outside. If she ignored it, were they likely to go away? She thought not but knew that she could not move Jem. She went downstairs to open the door.

"Wait a minute. I'm coming."

The thumping on the door continued and she heard shouting outside.

Jem cried out in agony when his mother's hands left him. His twisting, writhing body finally stilled and he rose from the bed. He looked around the familiar room but she was not there. Voices came from the floor below: loud voices, raised in anger. He was soon standing by his Ma and placed himself in between her and the soldier who was using his bayonet to force his way into the house.

"Leave her alone and get out of our house before I kill you." Jem yelled at the soldiers, even though there were two of them.

The soldiers ignored him and pushed past them both, stomping up the stairs with hardly another word. Ruth and Jem followed, powerless as the rooms were searched.

"In here," one of the soldiers called out to the other.

It was Ruth's turn to push past, whatever the consequences, although they almost stood aside to let her through. She rushed to the bedside and threw herself over the figure lying there, determined to protect him. The soldier moved away from the door and signalled to the other,

"Leave her be. That rebel's no threat."

To Jem's amazement, they walked to the stairs and left the house quietly. Ruth hardly noticed them go as she held onto the cold body of her son, tears streaming down her ravaged face. Jem reached out to her with comfort as his being flooded with waves of her grief but she could not feel his touch or the warmth of his love in her hour of need. She had lost her baby, her youngest child and she could see his life flashing past her own eyes as his body was gripped by the embrace of death.

Footsteps were heard on the stairs and Jem wondered if the soldiers had returned. It was Noah with the doctor but they quickly realised that they were too late. Noah saw his mother still holding onto Jem's body and his eyes filled with tears. She had made him promise to look after Jem and to bring him back to her. Jem was at home, but he was dead. Noah wished that it had been him lying lifeless on the bed. That would be easier than coping with her grief and his own guilt.

Jem was filled with sorrow for his brother and touched by the love he had shown. If only Noah knew he was all right, that he had survived death, his pain would be so much less. Noah's responsibility as a widow's only son would weigh heavy and she might not really forgive him for encouraging Jem to fight at Lexington on that fateful morning. Jem was being pulled away from them but found it hard not to stay close to their pain. The doctor slipped quietly away and left the family to grieve, as the soldiers had done.

As Jem moved away, his thoughts turned to his own situation. He hadn't thought about death before and hardly knew what to think now. Would he be a ghost, linked to the house and the sorrow of Noah and Ma? He would happily watch over them but hated the fact that he could not help them, that they didn't even know he was there. Even as the thoughts floated across his mind, he saw that there was another way forward.

The darkness of the small room was filled with a light of exceptional brightness and he knew that it held the answers.

A figure more familiar from photos than life could be seen in the distance, motioning him into the light. Jem did not have to think for a moment. With a deep wave of love, still mixed with sadness, he took a last look at the small woman and her minuteman son. Striding into the light, Jem felt overwhelmed with love; he knew with certainty that he had made his father proud.

THE END OF THE TRAIL

He walked into 'Jed's Place' (the only saloon in town), looking around for the others but it was deserted. He'd heard that Jed was long gone but it was still in business, taken over by Lance, Jed's barman, who was a good sort. Despite the new owner, there was a distinct lack of the necessary: customers. It looked much the same as always, except for the noise; it was as quiet as the grave. He'd waited months to get there and now this! He was trying to decide what had happened, when there was a grating noise behind him. His hand went to his holster, as he swung round to see the unmistakable figure of Marty B better known as 'Rattlesnake.'

"Folks have left town, or they're laid low, least the ones with sense. Me and the boys are planning a shoot out. Should be quite a party. You're welcome to stay and join us. Last I heard, you were a mean hand with a gun yourself."

Rattlesnake smiled at the thought of the night ahead. He kicked a chair out of the way and stood at the bar. He placed his gun carefully in front of him and caressed it with a look that some men would have reserved for a woman.

"Like to have it where I can see it. Now, you pour us a drink and we'll be just like old friends. Neat whiskey's fine. Just keep your hands where I can see 'em and we'd better have your gun on the bar with mine. I ain't had practice with drawing two for a while now."

Abel moved slowly to oblige but wondered if he could take out the Rattlesnake before the Snake decided he was bored with the company. He found two glasses and put a shot in each. He sent one across the bar for the Snake and tossed the other in the creature's face. Snake grabbed at his gun but before he could take aim, he was face up on the floor, a mass of blood. Abel glanced down.

"Not a pretty sight!" he said aloud and picked up the Snake's gun. A door creaked behind him and he wheeled round, ready to shoot again. The door opened slowly and he was joined by the owner of the saloon, who he knew well.

Lance went straight to the whiskey and put the bottle on the bar.

"You'd better drink it this time, reckon you've earned it!"

Abel nodded and poured a stiff drink which he drained in one.

"Fill it up again. Hardly notice the first one after a killing. Think we can do something with this low life?"

Lance pushed the bottle towards Abel but his eyes were fixed on the body.

"Better drag him out back. He said his friends were on their way; he'd only spoil the party."

Abel took another swig of whiskey before attempting to remove the Snake. When the gunman was gone and the floor mopped, the only trace of trouble was the new bullet hole in the bar where the Snake's gun had fired too late.

Abel still needed to know what was going on. He'd never seen the town like this and he doubted that it was just 'Snake and friends'.

"So what's happened?" He took another drink, although he had the feeling that he was going to need his wits about him.

Lance went to look out into the street and pulled the grimy curtains over the windows before he felt safe enough to explain.

"We've had a group of rustlers around for a time now and Stacey's men over at the old Evan's place decided they'd had enough. When they finally caught up with the trouble, it turned out that the whole operation was run by Macreadie. He was using Snake and his low life friends as muscle. War broke out, worse I've seen around these parts since the Rebs came up. Macreadie got more hired help, must have been making a fortune out of the rustling for years (always wondered where he got all his money!). Stacey and the boys didn't stand a chance. Cemetery filled faster than a whore house on a Saturday. Undertaker was the happiest man in town, cracking his face with a smile by the minute, on the sly, o' course."

Abel pushed the whiskey away wondering if he'd had too much already. Before he'd had time to turn from the bottle, the peace was shattered by the sound of gunfire coming from the street outside. Lance twitched the curtains.

"They're in town again. Don't think they need whiskey but I guess they'll be heading our way."

He looked even paler than before and wiped his face to get rid of the cold sweat.

Abel walked over to the window, to get a look at the problem. First, there was nothing but the noise of gunfire, but then he saw the horses. They were ridden at speed through the town; their riders were firing shotguns into the air, whooping and hollering. He wondered how many bullets they had and whether one had his name on it. Emmie flashed through his mind and his little girl (how Mary-Lou had grown); would he ever see them again? There was no time for reminiscing, he had to get organised for a fight or a quick getaway. He rushed to the back window and tried to see if there was any movement around the old barns. Lance had read his mind.

"You could get outa town quick. Might be best, 'specially if they find old Snake there."

Abel knew it was his best chance but he wasn't a coward and he didn't want to leave Lance to fight his battle.

"Wanna come? We could chance it. Might be better than dying here."

Lance looked as though he was really thinking about the proposition, but he walked over to Abel shaking his head.

"I sunk all my money into this place. It ain't much but it's all I've got. I reckon I gotta stay here and see it out, whatever happens. There's nothin' else for me. You don't have to be around though. I didn't shoot the Snake and I can serve the drinks. You won't have a chance unless you finish the lot of 'em."

Abel knew he was right. It was fight or run, never an easy choice for an old gun-slinger. The temptation to find out if he was still as good as he had been in the old days had to be balanced with the desire to survive and above all to see Emmie and Mary-Lou again.

They'd be waiting for him, as ever, at the end of the long trail and he'd promised that it would be the last time he'd drove cattle. They'd settle down and start the little homestead they'd always wanted; small, but just enough to get by and that was all he needed if he had them. There was a lot of romance about driving cattle, nights under the stars and days riding plains that seemed to stretch for ever. Yes, it had its moments but really it was a group of tired, sweaty men grinding out an existence, counting the days to the end of the trail and the chance to carry on living. They did it for the money, but strangely enough, it did have a way of getting under your skin, so it was hard to finally give it up, just like gun fighting. He loved the thrill of being first to the draw; he knew that the fastest would usually hit the target. There were no second chances and he'd liked it that way for such a long time, when it didn't matter if he lived or died, but that was before he'd met Emmie and before they'd had Mary-Lou. Now, he had a reason to get out of this miserable town and back to life again. Still, he had proved with Snake that he was fast; maybe as fast as before.

Abel's thoughts were interrupted by a crash ; the door swung open with so much force it barely stayed on its hinges. There was no decision to make now, it had been made for him. Now, he had to fight. If he ran, it would mean a bullet in the back; that was no way to die. His hand went to his holster but he did not draw his gun. There was a fine line between self defence and being hanged for murder.

When the voice came, he recognised it. Smiley Evans was a tall, thin, hungry-looking gunslinger, who was given his name because he was always happy and smiling, 'specially when he was killing, which as it happens was his favourite occupation.

"Well, I never! Abel James! Who'd 'a thought you'd be back in these parts. I'd heard you'd settled down. Can't remember who told me but looks like they were wrong. Let's have a drink for old times sake. Me and the boys are in town to have a good time and to look for our friend Snake. Don't suppose you've seen him? Remember Snake? Sure you do; everyone knows the Snake."

Abel didn't answer the question but guessed that he wasn't meant to. The grin on Smiley's face could only mean trouble. He was sure there'd be scattered bodies around the town and no-one left to testify against him or his friends. Smiley had carried on, obviously used to not getting a response.

Lance had taken up his position behind the bar, standing in front of the whiskey, almost as if he could protect it, which of course he could not. Smiley glanced at him and motioned towards a half-empty bottle.

"Two glasses, one for my old friend, Abel. You know, I haven't seen him around for years."

Lance poured the drinks and pushed them towards Smiley. He did not turn his back and could not stop the beads of cold sweat from dripping down his nose. Smiley noticed the familiar signs of fear and his grin broadened. There was no doubt he was a man who enjoyed what he did. Turning towards Abel, Smiley knew that the barman would not be fast enough to shoot him before he reached for his gun. Abel, however was another matter; he was a threat. Smiley motioned to Abel to take the drink, which he slid down the bar towards the man who had not spoken. Abel moved forward slowly, knowing that sudden movements were to be avoided; nervous gunslingers were notoriously fast on the trigger. He didn't feel like another drink and knew it would do little to help his reactions but refusing Smiley's offer was not an option. He took the drink in his left hand, leaving his right hand close to his side. The drink had hardly touched his lips, when the door to the back opened and another of the rustlers appeared.

"Hey, Smiley, I found Snake out back. He sure looks good, for a dead man. Got a bullet clean through the head."

Smiley ignored his friend, but stared at Abel with a glint in his eye.

"So you did meet Snake after all. I thought he'd be in here. Loved his drink, did our Snake, always found him in the saloon."

Before Smiley reached for his gun, there were two bursts of fire; he fell forward onto the side of the bar and then slumped to the floor with blood running across the smile on his face. The man in the doorway crashed into a nearby chair, as a bullet passed through his chest. Abel had certainly not lost his touch. He was as sharp as ever. But Abel was also lying face down ; he had a bullet in his back. Lance looked towards the door and saw Macreadie standing with a smoking shotgun. Reaching under the bar, Lance found his handgun; he drew it as quickly as he knew how and hit Macreadie in the chest. As the rifle fell and Macreadie blocked the doorway, Lance steadied himself and then bent to throw up behind the bar.

Abel hadn't realised at first that he had been hit. The euphoria of taking out two rustlers at once swept over him and he felt the warmth of success. When the pain flared through his back, he was surprisingly slow to understand what had happened. He noticed a body in front of him lying across the bar ; there was a familiar look about it but he could not see the face and he was still reeling with the shock of a shoot out. Somehow the room seemed misty, like one of those new-fangled cameras in soft focus. Apart from the body in front of him, Abel was not aware of the remainder of the bar and his memory was becoming hazy. What had happened? What was going on? As he looked more closely at the body, a chill recognition swept over him. It couldn't be, could it? Oh no, how could he have been so stupid, of course it was, it was him! It was obvious to anyone with half a brain. He was dead; but how had it happened? After all, he'd taken both the rustlers out; he was sure he had. He still couldn't focus on the whole room, but he had to know what had happened. He remembered Lance and wondered if he was all right. He'd sure been nervous; Abel could remember the cold sweat on Lance's face and Smiley's look of scorn when he noticed, but then he was used to seeing fear. Thinking of Lance, he became aware of the barman, who was over by the door. He was pulling something across the floor with some difficulty; it was a body. Looking closer, he realised it was Macreadie: a dead Macreadie. Lance was struggling with the bulky body and Abel reached out to give him a hand, before remembering that he was himself dead and could not do anything to help.

As his awareness grew, Abel started to notice the others; the souls who were also coming to terms with their situation. His predominant feeling was shock and a slow, quiet realisation, but he could sense the anger that filled the room: a leaden atmosphere of barely suppressed rage. Not surprisingly, dead gunslingers were no more sweet tempered than their living counterparts. Snake, Smiley and Macreadie had gravitated towards each other in their fury. They swept towards him; their overriding hope, to achieve together what they thought they had failed to manage alone. Abel turned to face them, but he was smiling, fuelling their anger. Abel knew that they could not kill him. He was already dead and he had a strong sense that there was little they could do to harm him in other ways. He found himself surrounded by them; they were pressing in towards his shade.

"James!"

Snake shouted his name and tried to throw a punch which went right through him. The others tried the same, striking out with futile fists which made contact but passed through him, as before. Abel stood firm and let the fists meet his ghost. But his whole being felt tremors of angry pain passing through, so that he struggled to show no reaction. As his mind flickered with shock, they appeared encouraged and tried again, lashing out at the man before them. He forced the pain away with the strength of his mind, blanking out the anger. Macreadie flinched and Abel realised that they too must have felt the pain of anger in this new state of being.

Eventually, they retreated to the corner of the room, their own pain thresholds overtaken.

Meanwhile, in the world of the living, another person had appeared in the saloon.

"Heard the shots and thought you might need some assistance." The undertaker surveyed the scene with grim satisfaction.

Lance looked up from the whiskey he had poured to steady his nerves and nodded.

"You're not wrong Jeremiah. You can do what you like with these four; in fact there could be a reward on any of them. But Abel, over here, well, I'd like the parson to say a few words over him in the graveyard and I think he's got folks over in Coatestown, so I reckon I'll send a telegraph to let them know. If it hadn't been for Abel, you'd be carrying me out to put in a box."

Jeremiah stood over Abel's body and put his hand into one of his jacket pockets. He took out a sepia photo and saw a young woman and a child with fair curls looking back at him.

"Mighty fine-looking woman and a pretty little girl."

He handed the photo to Lance who shook his head sadly and put it in his own pocket.

Abel had observed this exchange and it brought him away from the battle with the rustlers, who had not re-emerged from their dark corner. He had also looked again at the photo, which brought back thoughts of Emmie and Mary-Lou. Feeling their grief, the sobbing of his wife and the night -screams of his child consumed him with sadness. If a shade could have cried real tears, Abel would have filled buckets of emotion; he was flooded with guilt, knowing that he should have ridden straight home rather than stopping off to meet his death. What could he have been thinking, riding into this place? Worse, why did he stay? The pain and grief engulfed him with darkness and the room filled with a fog of despair. He was pulled down and felt a weight around his ghostly heart. Across the room, a voice echoed, although he couldn't be sure what was said.

Lance's words, though indistinct, brought a glimmer of warmth to the cold, dark place Abel had drifted to. The friendship of the camp fire, long nights of shared stories and making do, even when rations were low, answered his own question about the reason he had ridden into town. Looking ahead through the mist, he could see figures which grew larger as they advanced. His friends had met their fate nearby at the same hands. In death, the power of thought was potent and he was drawn to them. Abel reached out and felt their friendship pull him from the dark. He knew that he had been lucky to have known them and to have had the precious time with Emmie and Mary-Lou. Love filled his being and blocked all his negative thoughts. Even the sadness of loss could not stop the overwhelming wave of love which drove him towards his friends.

Once within the group, he felt stronger and still energised by the warmth of love. He became aware, as they all did that there was a light ahead. His own awareness of the room where he had met his death had been fading. And now, all that seemed to fill the space was the strength of the light. As one, they moved towards it, knowing it was the only thing they could do. It was the unknown and like the trail, it went on and on: for ever.

SPION KOP

The ball flew across the face of the goal. It landed at the feet of a red-shirted player, who thumped it into the back of the net. The crowd roared its delight; what a great win this was going to be!

"Right boys, we're off. We'll be up that hill in no time."

Albert woke up with a start. How he'd managed to doze standing up he didn't know but it was good to be back in Liverpool, even if it was only in his head. Now they were advancing again. The poor bloody infantry just did as they were told and today's orders were to chase the Boers off Spion Kop. He hoped it would be as good as its name and the 'Spy Hill' would give them some good views of the South African landscape and the enemy.

"Good sleep, Albert?" Sid laughed as they set off. "Sorry we had to wake you. I'll send the butler round next time to run your bath and bring you a cup of tea!"

Albert grinned and joined in the joke.

"Make sure the water's nice and hot. He can give me a shave as well."

The thought of a hot bath and shave was almost as good as his dream. The one place this lousy war couldn't get was in your head. If you escaped into your mind, you just about kept your sanity. At least that was what he believed. Course, you had to keep your wits about you when the fighting began and when the sargeant was around.

The regiment headed towards the hill and started to climb. A thick mist hung over the hill, so that Albert could hardly see in front of him. He could hear firing up ahead, which added to the confusion.

"What's going on, Sid?" He could barely see his friend but a voice came through the fog and bullets.

"The Boers are on the run, Albie. A bit of success for once."

Albert couldn't believe his ears. It was an easy victory; well, didn't that make a change!

They went on up the hill, firing whenever they sensed movement, although the South African Boers seemed to evaporate just like the mist into the night.

"That was the best night's work we've had since we came over," laughed Albert, leaning on his rifle.

"'Bout time too! Maybe our luck's on the turn. Had to happen, a fine fighting force like this was always going to sort this lot out. Mark my word, we'll finish 'em off and be back home to cheer the Reds on in the cup, you'll see!"

Sid took out a Woodbine and felt around his pockets for a match. Albert drifted off into dreams of home again. What a day that would be, marching up to Wembley instead of up an African hill. Perhaps facing an army of Everton blue, not a khaki army of Dutch Boers. A far superior battle to be sure, a Merseyside derby and he'd still be on the winning side!

After the easy victory, even the sargeant looked pleased for once. Well, there was a first time for everything!

"Bed time boys. Sappers are on the way. We'll finish the job tomorrow that's for sure, when this fog lifts. Let's dig in for the night. This'll do nicely to set us up for the advance."

He disappeared into the fog and Sid reluctantly put out his cigarette and moved aside as the Royal Engineers started to dig into the unforgiving ground.

"Come on, Albie, wake up. The sappers are coming through to help us dig in. Looks like we will have time to rest after all. God knows we need it."

He threw his kit bag at Albie who managed to duck out of the way, waking quickly and leaving behind his images of Liverpool glory. Instead, the bag was caught in the nick of time and Albie began to dig into the dusty soil. The hard ground made the task a back-breaking struggle for the Engineers, perhaps the Boers had been wise to leave this unforgiving terrain to their enemies. The land would undermine the strength of the army even if they could not. How many times had armies been defeated by the land or the climate?

Eventually, the order came to stop digging. The sappers had made little progress but it was judged enough to provide cover for the night. After all, they were on a hill which would provide a good vantage point the next day. The soldiers were exhausted and a much-needed rest was in order before the campaign could continue. Sid and Albert slumped down with the others, heads laid on their kitbags, as comfortable as any feather pillow to the shattered men.

"Reckon we'll sleep tonight, Albie." Sid's lips uttered the words but his eyes closed and he did not hear Albie's reply.

They slept soundly, despite the stony ground, until the early morning light caused them to stir. Albert had been far away in pleasant dreams once more, walking Liverpool streets leading to home in Varthen Street and drinking in the nearby Albert pub, his namesake. He had just lifted a pint glass and wondered why his lips felt so dry. When he opened his eyes, life flooded over him again with all its disappointment and despair. *That was a dream, but this is a nightmare,* he thought. Still, he had to get on with it, get it over with and then there would be happier times at home again. At least he was with his Scouse mates; they were in it together. Even in the early morning the heat was oppressive and the urge to drink water unrelenting. He remembered that supplies were running out. They needed to get a move on, get down this infernal hill and find some more liquid for their parched mouths. Water would taste better than a pint of Mild and Albie never thought he would ever think such a thing! Certainly, the fog had lifted and this made the heat from the sun all the stronger. Still, it shouldn't be long before they'd be off across the hills and over to relieve Ladysmith just as they had been ordered. Maybe then they'd get some R and R with a bit of decent grub and hot water to wash away the dust which appeared to be part of them. Albie couldn't remember what he looked like, or what it felt like to be clean. The smell didn't bother him but the feel of grit and dirt in every crevice of his body was gradually getting him down. The jokes, at first a help, weren't funny any more; he'd had enough; time to go home, the sooner, the better.

All the thoughts crowding into his mind were overtaken by the loud sound of battle. A bombardment had begun, but where was it coming from? They were supposed to be on top of the hill, surveying the scene at a great advantage over the enemy. It should be an easy stroll from here; that's what they had worked so hard to achieve in the past twenty-four hours, wasn't it? Artillery and rifle fire rained down on them (yes, down on them!). They were obviously not at the top.

Like the others, Albie reached for his rifle and tried to shield himself by lying in the trench. Around him the noise of battle was punctured by the screams of dying men. Where could he shoot? He couldn't see clearly in the heat of the sun and the panic of the attack. The firing was definitely coming from higher up in the Rangeworthy Hills; they were trapped like sitting ducks with no way out at all.

Albie heard a dull groan and saw a splash of blood as Sid slumped down almost on top of him. There was no doubt Sid was gone and had in fact saved his Scouse mate from the bullets as he died. Albie's rifle was running out of bullets and he had to try to get more ammunition if he was going to stand a chance. He felt round Sid's body to see if he could grasp his rifle which was no longer needed. He felt the smooth metal, hot from the heat and sticky with his friend's blood. Wiping his hands quickly on his jacket, he prayed that Sid had some ammo. He was in luck and he fired with all the passion he could muster. If he was going to die, he would take a few Boers with him. There was nothing else to do.

For a moment the shooting seemed to stop. Up ahead, he could see white handkerchiefs raised on sticks and soldiers started to stand up in the trench and walk towards the firing. A voice came from the distance.

"No surrender! Do you hear? No surrender! We fight on. I'll kill you myself if I have to. Any man who surrenders is a deserter."

At that, the firing started again and the men appeared to fall back into the trench. Albie fired the rifle until the bullets stopped and he collapsed in exhaustion and desperation. He would have to find another rifle or at least the spare bullets from his bag. Moving was not easy and reloading would be hard. His eyes searched the dust and bodies around him, eventually noticing a rifle butt under a twisted body not far away. He inched himself carefully over mangled remains until he was in a better position to reach for the gun. The sound of artillery deafened him so much, he felt he could hardly think but he concentrated on the rifle and slid his arm towards it. A flash nearby dazed him for a second and he felt pain surging through his whole being.

The summer battlefield was black silence: frozen time.

He was sitting on the front step polishing the biggest conker he'd ever seen (it was going to be a winner); he was playing leapfrog in the street with his mates but falling off Paddy Riley's back and landing at the feet of Father O'Hare, who'd just come out of 'The Albert'; sitting in the kitchen when Mam told him and Vic that Mary was getting married; hanging round Anfield on match day, watching the crowds and then listening for the roar when Liverpool scored a goal; going through the turnstiles for the first time, early to get at the front; hearing the thud of the ball and the shouts of the players on the pitch; cheering 'til his throat was sore when the final whistle blew and the team had won; kissing Mam and giving her a hug and Pa a handshake as the flags waved and he left for the war; the dust, blood and bullets moving in a haze amid the comradeship forged by pain and suffering. The images moved across his mind in those fleeting moments when life drained from his body.

Looking down on 'the murderous acre', Albie could see that there had been little chance of survival. Over two hundred bodies lay in the trench alone, so the hill was a confusion of souls coming to terms with their demise, groaning wounded and survivors still fighting but taken back down the hill in retreat, even though the Boers themselves had given up. A wave of sorrow and frustration washed over him, as he knew that, having won the battle, the British had left the hill and it was all for nothing. They had failed and it would be re-taken by the Boers.

His death was pointless, not a blaze of glory in victory but a futile sacrifice. Poor leadership had led men into a blind alley of death; they had walked into a trap because no-one knew the terrain. He felt no release in death but only despair that it had all been for nothing. He looked around and became more aware of the others, Sid among them, who had not recovered from the shock of death and the knowledge of survival. They could see their broken bodies below them and knew with certainty that they were casualties of battle but they could still see and feel, albeit in a very different way.

The physical pain had gone but the pain of emotion was great and pulled them into the darkness that surrounded a place where they had committed the greatest sin, that of taking the life of another. Of course, it had not been of their choosing; they had just been following orders and fighting for their country. They were brothers in arms and yet their greatest realisation was the futility of war and its horror. They were a long way from home, fighting for the cause of empire, rather than a personal crusade. Although it had been a bright day, the souls sensed a darkness as black as night, reflecting the pain and grief of suffering. Yet, there was no hatred; they were just pawns in a game, bearing no malice for their enemies, who were at least fighting for their own land. The British soldiers had no choice, the whole thing seemed futile now but death was a fact. This led them away from the despair. It was sadness rather than hatred and so it was possible for the souls to rise above the dark gloom to find hope.

Albie found Sid and the others; they embraced with a stream of comfort and healing which banished the blackest darkness. This moved them away from the trench on top of the hill and they found the dead Boers also suffering the same confusion and adjustment. The Boers were passionate about the fight for the freedom and control of their land but now they would not see any rewards and they wondered if they had really died for nothing. Would the war be won in the end?

Tentatively, Albie, Sid and the others approached the men who had been their enemies and put out their hands in reconciliation. The Boers turned away in anger at first, some even trying to strike out at the peacemakers. Gradually, a number of the Boers returned the handshakes and were able to rise above the destructive emotion of war and the dark despair of the battlefield.

"Somehow, everyone looks the same in death, friend and foe," observed Albie.

Those who were ready to leave some of their pain behind, noticed a brighter light than day ahead. It suffused them and they were drawn away from the bloody battlefield towards peace. For Albie and Sid, it was not Liverpool but it was indeed home.

At Anfield, after their 2nd League Championship in the 1905-6 season, Liverpool re-named the Walton Breck end of the ground 'Spion Kop' in honour of the Scouse supporters who had died. Albie thought it was a fitting memorial, there in the place where he had lived his dreams. Looking on from the afterlife, the dead of Spion Kop were able to glory in the passion of that special place, knowing that their sacrifice would never be forgotten.

IN SERVICE:
MAID IN HEAVEN

Mary opened tired eyes and squinted at the little bedside clock (a present from her family back home in Ireland). Five o'clock, still dark, but time to get up nonetheless. How she would have liked to turn over in bed-just this once; it was, of course out of the question. She poked a toe out from under the blankets: freezing! Suddenly, the bedclothes were torn away from her.

"Come on lazybones, you've got the fires to do!"

"Oh, it's freezing Ethel. I hate getting up!"

Ethel knew exactly what Mary meant but was rather better at getting started in the morning than her friend. This morning however, Mary had a good reason for being slow. She felt quite ill, although she was anxious not to show it. She splashed the icy water onto her skin in an attempt to wake herself up and felt better, but she was soon rushing along the dark corridor to the privy, where she bent over the bowl retching with sickness.

Having been sick, Mary felt a little better, so when Mrs Bright, the cook, offered buttered toast, she accepted it with a thank you and tried her best to eat.

Mrs Bright was a kind old stick, all heart really, a bit gruff at times, but only when she was rushed and in a tizz. She was at her best early in the day, before the occupants of the house had risen and last thing at night, when most were in their beds fast asleep. At these times in the castle that was her kitchen, she reigned supreme and purred contentment.

Mrs Bright cast a searching look across at her young maid. "Now, Mary, when you've done the fires, come back here and you can take a tray to M'lady. I've got her some nice fresh eggs and freshly baked bread. Just the thing for someone in her condition. Do mind you're quick about it. Mabel's ill this morning. Rather too much of my rich trifle last night in my opinion. Silly girl's eyes are bigger than her stomach if you ask me."

Mary's face fell, though she dared not complain. How she would manage the fires in time, feeling as she did, she couldn't imagine. The wrath of Mrs Bright was too much to contemplate. She would just have to do her best.

Despite feeling rather 'off colour' all morning, Mary laid the fires and returned to the kitchen for the breakfast tray. Mrs Bright was grateful and promised her a rock cake as a special treat.

"Well, I never, M'lady has insisted there should be no eggs, only toast and marmalade, and those eggs new laid this morning!"

Mary said little, only taking the tray with a nod. Ever since the mistress of the house had been with child, she had been most changeable. Of course, every whim and craving was catered for. How she wished someone would look after her until the time came to have her baby.

Mary's situation had dawned slowly as she noticed the signs (or lack of them). The morning sickness which was now a regular occurrence confirmed her worst fears. She had told no-one. Although, lying in the darkness of her bed at night, she wondered what her baby would be like;

this little boy-she was so sure- who would be a future heir to the large estate in which he had been conceived. She imagined how she would tell Algie and how thrilled he would be -after all, he'd said how much he loved her – really he had.

Even if M'lady had a boy, Algie was the first in line, and then his son. Of course, when they knew about her baby, they would be shocked at first, but it would be all right, once they got used to the idea. After all, they had always been so nice to her and she had been treated with so much kindness ever since she had arrived from Ireland six months ago. She'd never been away from home before and she was so homesick.

"This is your home now," M'lord had said and she had felt so much better, especially when Algie had said such nice things to her and paid her so many compliments.

Approaching the bedroom door, Mary knocked rather timidly. No answer came, so she was forced to knock again, a bit louder. This time, a faint voice could be heard and so she entered the room quietly.

"Mary, just put the tray on the table by the window. I really don't feel like food this morning. I know Mrs Bright goes to so much trouble. Please tell her I ate it and come back for the tray when she has her mid- afternoon break. Our little secret?"

Mary tried to smile,

"Of course M'lady. I'll come up later."

Looking at the breakfast, Mary could feel the sickness returning. She understood exactly what the mistress meant.

On her way to the kitchen, Mary resolved to share her secret at last. It would be comforting to be able to talk about it and to have someone caring for her a little before she found the opportunity to tell Algie. The chance to speak to him would come soon enough. She had overheard Mrs Bright saying that he was coming down from Oxford with friends for the weekend. He would be bound to seek her out and she could tell him her exciting news. Before then, she would explain her circumstances to Ethel. Practical Ethel would be a great help. How lucky she was to share a room with such a friend!

Her mind made up, Mary could hardly wait until bedtime. The rest of the day seemed to pass so slowly but eventually they lay quietly in the dark.

"Ethie, are you awake? I've got something to tell you." Mary couldn't see, but she thought it would be easier that way.

"Course, I'm not asleep, Mary. You are funny, we've only just come to bed. What's wrong?"

Mary took a deep breath.

"There's nothing wrong. Well, not really. It's just that...I'm, well, I'm going to have a baby."

Ethel gasped in horror and sat straight up in bed despite the dark. She fumbled for a match, lit the candle and went to sit on Mary's bed.

"Oh, no, Mary! When? Who? Oh, no, not Algie? Please tell me it's not Algie?"

This was not the response that Mary had expected or hoped for.

"Why not Algie, Ethel?"

Ethel was regretting having said anything about Algernon, but knew that she would have to explain herself.

"The last maid I shared with, Gladys (before you), was packed off home quickly. Everyone said she was pregnant."

The candlelight caught Mary's whitened face and the young maid felt sickness rising again, even though it was not morning.

"That can't be true, it can't. You don't know! You really don't know!" She cried out wildly and dissolved in tears. Ethel reacted kindly.

"No, Mary, of course I don't know definitely. Maybe it was all talk and rumour. After all, she left suddenly, so we never really knew for certain."

This reassurance calmed Mary and slowly, her tears were dried. She tried to summon the courage to rebuff Ethel's comments.

"I'll see Algie. He'll be pleased. Everything will be fine. You'll see. He's home this weekend."

She replied weakly, desperately trying to convince herself.

Mary struggled through the remainder of the week, waiting nervously for Algie's return to the house. Her happy imaginings gave way to worries, as she accepted that her news might not be received with rapture.

Friday was a busy day, with Mrs Bright planning weekend meals for a house full of guests. Mary was needed to help prepare vegetables in the kitchen. She seemed to have peeled potatoes till her hands were sore and as soon as one job was completed, Mrs Bright thought of another.

Late in the afternoon, Mrs Bright took a tray down from the shelf and turned to Mary, who had just finished the carrots and swede.

"Mary, wash your hands. Take up some tea and scones to the library. Master Algernon is there with some guests. He always loves my scones, especially with my special strawberry jam ; I've still got the odd pot tucked away."

Mary's heart fluttered; she would see him again. He wouldn't be able to say much (not being alone), but he would see her and no doubt find a way to meet her on her own. Glad to leave the vegetables, she assembled the tray of scones carefully and carried it out into the hall, taking deep calming breaths.

Even before she got to the library door, Mary could hear laughter. Balancing the tray with some difficulty, she knocked a little quietly. There seemed to be no answer, although she could still hear voices and indeed laughter within. There was nothing to be done but to enter. Mary pushed the door open and went in...A stifled noise came from the far corner of the library.

"Oh, Algie," someone giggled, "you are so wicked."

Algie was locked in an embrace with a young lady who was pretending to push him away. Hearing the door, he retreated, though too late to avoid being seen.

"Er, ...thank you Mary. Just put it over there would you?"

Algie got to his feet with some difficulty and moved away from the sofa they had been occupying. He attempted to straighten his tie and stole a quick glance in the fireplace mirror to see if his face looked as red as it felt.

"Come on Grace. Have some scones; they really are Mrs Bright's speciality."

Mary's hands were shaking but she managed to put the tray down and then left the room as quickly as she could. Closing the door, she heard the young woman's voice.

"Now, now, Algie, not in front of the servants!"

Mary stopped and leaned back on the door.

"That's all I am, a servant. How could I think it would be different?" she mumbled to herself. All at once, Mary realised how foolish she had been. The very idea that Algie could have been in love with her seemed quite ridiculous. A shiver ran through her body and she felt sick; not morning sickness this time, instead it was the feeling of her whole world collapsing around her. She steadied herself, clutching onto a low polished table in the hall, despite the finger-marks she knew she would leave.

The library door opened and the young lady (if indeed she was), ran lightly past her, stifling a giggle; her hand was pushed over her mouth to try to mask repeated hiccups.

Standing straight and with uncharacteristic bravery, Mary re-entered the library to find Algernon. He was slumped in the deep leather sofa once again, facing a large gin and tonic, to which he had become rather partial, even early in the day.

"We haven't finished yet, Mary. You don't need to take the plates. We're having a little drink first."

Mary stood facing him, looking down at the dissolute figure. She wondered what she had ever seen in him, but she was determined to go on.

"I've come to talk to you, Algie, to tell you something."

His glazed eyes hardly registered her tone and he laughed, picking up the glass as if in a toast.

"You're a real sport, Mary and you're looking 'specially lovely, you know. Perhaps we could meet up later, when everyone's gone to bed?"

With a sharp intake of breath, Mary continued,

"I'm going to have a baby, Algie. It's your baby."

Algie laughed, but it was a nervous, shaking laugh and his words brought no comfort, as deep inside she knew they would not.

"You're a pretty girl; you must have lots of admirers and you know how to have a good time."

He gulped the gin. "Anyway, there are people who can get it sorted. I'll make some enquiries, if you like. Just as a favour you understand; as a friend. I won't tell anyone. I know you wouldn't like to lose your position here and it would upset Ma and Pa if they knew you'd let them down."

He tried to take her hand but she wrenched it away. Her eyes flickered down at the table and quick as lightning, she lifted the glass, flinging the drink into his face, just as a hiccup heralded the return of his young ladyfriend. Tears streamed down Mary's face as she ran from the room. Stopping in the doorway, she turned back and shouted,

"He's a liar and he's no gentleman."

That of course was the problem. A gentleman, Mary had thought would keep his word. A gentleman could be trusted, not like the boys she had grown up with, who fumbled with their girls in the haystacks without a thought of the consequences. In truth, most of those did right by the girls if they had to, albeit at the end of a shotgun when necessary. But a gentleman? Gentlemen had to be different, didn't they? All too late, Mary knew the answer. She was alone, disgraced; she would be thrown out of the house and sent home. Home? That was the last place she could go. They wouldn't want her or the baby. Nor could they afford another mouth to feed. She thought of her mother, forever on her knees in church. The shame would send her to an early grave; no, going home was not the answer.

Mary didn't know what to do but she had to get away for a few minutes. She needed to calm down before anyone asked her what was wrong and she had to have time to think. She knew the place to go; no-one would find her there. The views were lovely and it was so peaceful. She loved to escape, to be alone there when rare opportunities presented themselves. Although she knew she didn't want to speak to anyone else, she wondered how long it would be before someone would be looking for her. She was sure to get into trouble (as if she wasn't in enough already). Anger welled up inside her and soon, bitter tears flowed freely with the realisation that all her dreams were in ruins.

Mary rushed for the stairs in a panic that she would be seen and have to explain the state she was in. She climbed out of the small window that led to the roof terrace and was soon gazing over the rooftop through bleary eyes. She was beginning to feel better, when she heard laughter drifting up from the garden. It seemed unreal, floating past on the air through her torment. She peered over the parapet, to confirm her worst fears. Algie was fooling around with the giggling young woman. This time, it looked like hide and seek in the shrubbery.

"He's forgotten about me already," she sobbed, and then determined to attract his attention. She refused to let him forget her so easily. She leaned further over, trying to make him notice her. He was too preoccupied, and she was a long way up. An idea floated across her mind, as ideas do, although such ideas are best allowed to pass by. This one would not be cast aside so easily, the thought was attractive. Mary leaned a little further over contemplating the unthinkable. It was simple, just a little push form her sensible servant's shoes and she hurtled towards the ground. A rash moment and no chance to turn back. Her eyes, wide with panic, saw the gravel path, then a flash of intense pain and darkness.

The darkness cleared and she found herself looking up at an ashen-faced Algie. Well, she did not know how she had survived but he'd certainly noticed her. Somehow, she felt better. At least, she'd done something and now she felt strangely that there was nothing to worry about anymore. Algie would care about her, she knew he would. She waited for him to come to her, to help her, but horrified, she watched him put his arm around the young woman and turn away. The two disappeared into the house. She shouted out and went to follow them, determined that Algie would hear her but her attention was diverted by Mr Butterfield, the butler, who was running from the house, carrying a blanket. She turned round in confusion and watched as he covered up the body, which was lying broken, blood mingling with red rose petals scattered onto the path.

Slowly, Mary began to realise what had happened. It was obvious really. She had taken her own life and also that of her unborn child. She thought about the members of the household and found herself in the kitchen where Mrs Bright was ministering strong sweet tea to a distraught Ethel.

"It's a sad business. Of course, she'll go to Hell," Mrs Bright observed, crossing herself as she put down the teacup. Loud sobs came from Ethel in between slurps of tea.

"She was having a baby."

Mrs Bright took this as an opportunity to continue her train of thought.

"Well, I thought as much. No hope for her soul then. No better then she should be, that girl. And her poor parents over in Ireland, devout Catholics. What ever will they do? The shame of it..."

Mary sank into dark despair. She was pulled into a shadowy corner of the kitchen. Darkness closed round her with every despairing thought. A Catholic upbringing had made clear the fate awaiting suicides. Why had she been so stupid?

"I didn't mean to do it," she tried to tell Mrs Bright. "I just wanted Algie to notice me, to give him a scare. I didn't mean ... well, I suppose for a minute, I did, but then, it was too late."

She became aware of dark shapes nearby and accusing voices filled her head.

"You did mean it . You did it. Yes, it is too late. You are damned!"

They laughed and the hollow laughter consumed her whole being as she was pulled into the darkness of her own thoughts.

Ethel continued to sob, although a little more quietly and less frequently.

"I'll miss her. She was a good friend and she was not a bad girl. I won't have you say that about her, I won't!" she rounded on Mrs Bright fiercely, before another sob escaped and a tear dripped into her tea.

The words broke into the gloom, flickering with a warmth that crept into Mary's shade. The small glow expanded, fighting the sorrow. Mary strained through the dark mist to notice golden light around her friend. The sudden regret she felt at having caused this sadness almost pulled her back towards the cold darkness, but beyond Ethel she saw a powerful white light. She knew it was the way she wanted to go and yet she felt doubtful. If it was Heaven, she wouldn't be allowed in, would she? Even if she were, Judgement Day would surely send her into the eternal fires of Hell. Mrs Bright said so and everything she had grown up believing confirmed that this was true.

Ethel had calmed down with the tea. Practical as ever, she had an idea.

"Can we say a prayer for Mary? I think it might help, Mrs Bright, I really do."

Mrs Bright looked doubtful, her thoughts turning to the dinner she had to prepare but seeing the maid's pale tear-stained face, she softened,

"Well, all right, Ethel. If you like."

Ethel looked relieved, pleased to have something to do.

"Can I light a candle and say the words?" Ethel asked.

"Yes, yes," Mrs Bright responded, "but do hurry up. I have got to make dinner for a house-full. Tragedy has a way of making folk hungry."

Ethel lit the candle solemnly and they bowed their heads.

"Father, please forgive Mary for taking her own life and that of her baby. Save her from the fires of Hell. She was a good girl really and a good friend. Please take care of her and take her to Heaven- if you can. Amen"

Mary was touched by Ethel's prayer. She felt drawn once again towards her and then to the light. She decided to try to move towards it. Slowly, she made her way beyond the people in the room, until the light was the only thing she could see. Its brightness blotted out everything and stepping into it, she felt an overwhelming sense of love and forgiveness. A small blue light followed Mary and she remained close to it as she moved forward. Ahead she could see a smiling face. Her grandmother reached out towards her and Mary walked into her outstretched arms.

LADIES' DAY

Anna opened her eyes, squinting at the sun which streamed through the curtains.

That's the problem with going off to sleep staring at the stars, she thought. She would have liked to lie in her bed, enjoying the comforting warmth but she knew that she could not delay; there was so much to do. Anyway, it was better to be busy; lying in bed would only give her too much time to think and to change her mind. She had promised herself that there would be no backing down, although it would be easy; after all, no-one actually knew of her plan. At least, not her real plan.

She dressed quickly and rushed down to breakfast. Her father had left for the office and her mother was finishing her toast and marmalade.

"Are you going out today, darling?" Her mother raised her eyes over a china teacup.

"Yes, Mama. I'm meeting Emma and Mary." Anna tried to make her plans seem ordinary, although her chest felt tight inside and she was sure her voice trembled with nerves. Mrs Forbes- Cartwright only shook her head.

"Do take care, Anna. It *is* race day and everywhere will be so busy. Couldn't you leave it and meet up next week, when everything will be back to normal?"

Anna gave all the reassurances she could and escaped from the discomfort of the breakfast table after forcing herself to eat something, even though she felt quite sick.

Nevertheless, she couldn't stop herself from pausing at the door to look back at her mother, who seemed lost in her own thoughts again as she gazed out over the garden.

Anna blinked back a tear.

That won't do, she thought, turning away. Her resolve hardened and she ran up the stairs, grabbed her things and was out of the door with a quick shout of "Goodbye."

There would be no lingering farewells; her mind had been made up for an age. All that was left was to carry out her intentions and above all, not to let everybody down. Still, as she rushed to get her bicycle, she noticed her mother, who had come out into the garden. Waving her sunhat to catch Anna's attention, she called out.

"Ride carefully and have a lovely day."

Anna winced, but recovered herself enough to wave back before she cycled out of the driveway trying hard not to wobble and fall off.

Ascot, though usually quiet, was hectic on race days, especially when the royal party were among the race goers. Anna struggled through the crowds. How was she even going to find her friends? It was just madness!

Eventually, she noticed a familiar hat and the fiery red hair of Emma in the middle of a group queuing to get in to the course. Mary was with her, but her smaller figure did not stand out from the crowd. Anna failed to notice the large picnic basket that they held between them.

Emma caught sight of her friend who was walking, having left her bicycle behind the grocer's shop (thanks to the kindness of Mr Wilson).

"Anna, come on, we've been waiting for ages. Where have you been? We'll be through in a minute. The queue's just starting to move. Hurry up!"

Emma was not known for her patience and she did have a point. Anna managed to get through the crowd and they were soon inside the racecourse, with a good position by the rails.

There was plenty of time before the first race and the contents of the picnic basket were emptied. Dainty sandwiches, cheese, fruit cake and apple pies were spread out on a pretty blue cloth. For the second time that day, Anna had to force an appetite.

Emma and Mary seemed cheerful and determined to enjoy the food they had brought. Gradually the number of spectators increased and the noise reached fever pitch as cheers rang out around them. The royal party were approaching, much to everyone's excitement.

Their eyes flickered from face to face and Emma removed a tablecloth at the bottom of the basket. There, carefully concealed, were sashes and a large banner. Without doubt, Royal Ascot provided the perfect opportunity for a 'Votes for Women' protest.

"Here's the banner. You and Mary can hold it while I throw the leaflets into the carriage. We should just have time before the police arrest us. Make sure you turn towards the crowd so that everyone can see."

Although Emma thrust the banner towards her, Anna held back for a moment.

"Em, I don't want to go now. I'm going to wait until later, till the races."

Emma and Mary put on their sashes in disbelief. How could their friend let them down at the eleventh hour?

"We've planned this, Anna. We're going now. You're either with us or not, it's up to you."

Emma was determined. The protest would go ahead, with or without Anna.

The two young women climbed out onto the racecourse, just as the royal carriage came in sight. The cheers of the crowd grew louder as the King approached, but jeers rang out when the banner was unfurled and people realised that the royal party had been held up by a demonstration.

"Shame, shame!" could be heard echoing from the gentlemen in the stands.

The police were not far away. They rushed up to see what the commotion was all about and arrested Anna's friends without any resistance. They had completed their protest and were escorted from the ground, to be charged with disturbing the peace.

Unnoticed in the crowd, Anna stood frozen, her hand clutching the sash which she tried to hide. The protest had sent a ripple of surprise around the crowd but the King and his companions continued their procession and the races began almost on time.

Watching the first race, Anna checked the riders and the horses. Certainly, the crowd shouted loudest for the jockey wearing purple and scarlet -the royal colours.

The horses in the eagerly anticipated third race rounded the bend in the track and the crowd surged forward with deafening shouts. In the excitement, no-one noticed the slight figure who slipped through the fence and was soon in front of the galloping horses. The beat of hooves thundered in her ears and Anna's heart thumped faster and faster as the movement blurred and she felt the impact. For a moment, the shouts receded and the blackened world spun into oblivion.

The King's horse stumbled and the jockey, who had tried so hard to avoid the woman in his path, was unseated and curled up on the ground, trying to protect himself from the pounding hooves.

When her eyes opened, she was standing among the chaos of horses, some flying past, others falling in confusion.

I've failed, she thought in dismay. *I'm here. No-one will notice. It's all for nothing.*

There did seem to be a large number of people running onto the track.

This is it. I'll be arrested, just like the others and their protest was better. They disrupted the King and I couldn't even stop the race.

She could see the police, and prepared to face the consequences. Nevertheless, they passed her without comment. In a trance, she followed them, sure that they would arrest her soon enough. They were crowding round something on the track and it was difficult for her to see what it was. A path was cleared for a stretcher and she saw the reason for their indifference. A muddied, white sash lay on the turf; it was blood spattered but the words 'Votes for Women' were still clear enough to read; by its side lay the crumpled body of a young woman. Anna realised that she had been successful.

Another suffragette had died when she had thrown herself under the King's horse at the Derby, the year before. There were extra police at race courses for a while, but then the police were needed elsewhere, so numbers were reduced and, in truth, no-one thought that such an event was likely to occur again. Although there were a good number of 'bobbies' at Ascot, no doubt the newspapers would be up in arms and questions would be asked in Parliament as people came to terms with the events of the day.

Anna watched as her body was lifted onto the stretcher and carried away. Not knowing what else to do, she followed the police and watched as the body was taken away in an ambulance. The police went to a room where Emma and Mary were being held, so that the young women could be questioned about their friend. Mary collapsed in a swoon when she was told about Anna's death. After being revived with smelling salts, she sobbed uncontrollably when the police explained what had happened. Emma appeared angry as she spoke about Anna.

"She refused to come with us, to demonstrate. If she'd come, it would have been better and she would still be alive now."

Her face as red as her hair, she wrung her hands and tried hard to stifle the tears that were determined to escape from her eyes.

"Why didn't she listen to me? I had no idea she meant to …to…do …that. If I'd known, I'm sure I could have stopped her. How I wish…I…it's too late now, just too late. I'm so sorry."

Even the inspector appeared sympathetic for a moment, as he realised the obvious distress of the two well spoken young ladies in front of him, but he did not want to encourage criminals and was determined to uphold the rule of law.

"Well Miss, you can't change what has happened but you can help me to contact the young lady's family. Can you give me her name and address?"

Emma recovered herself enough to provide the information needed by the police and a police car was sent out to Anna's home.

As soon as Emma had mentioned her name, Anna's thoughts turned to her parents. Thinking about them, she found herself in the garden, where her mother was cutting roses for the house. Mrs Forbes-Cartwright clutched the fence post when she saw the police car enter the drive. Its presence could only mean bad news. She tried to steady herself, to keep a dignified control but had to be helped to a nearby garden seat when she was told of Anna's fate. The red roses fell onto the gravel path as if in remembrance and Anna felt the wrenching pain experienced by her mother. Cold grief gripped the heart of the woman who had waved so cheerfully only a few hours before. Anna had no idea it would be like this. She didn't know what she had thought. Her actions, which had seemed selfless in support of the emancipation of women, now seemed so utterly selfish when she saw the pain they had caused those who were dearest to her heart. Her mother was grief stricken and her father was still to face the terrible news when he returned home. Anna so wanted to put her arms around her mother and comfort her; to tell her that she had survived death. If only she could, surely that would make some difference.

Her mother asked no questions about how she had died. The fact that her daughter was no more seemed all that concerned her, yet the police explained the events of the day in full, despite the fact that the grieving woman seemed hardly able to take it all in. Having heard the long explanation, Mrs Forbes-Cartwright dabbed her eyes and looked directly at the police inspector. She took a deep breath and spoke quietly.

"My Anna always had principles. I'm not surprised that she fought for what she believed in. I'll always be proud of her."

Had Anna's shade been able to cry, she would have wept and wept. She was only thoughts and those pulled her painfully towards her devastated parent. At the same time, she could feel the warmth of the love expressed and deeply felt by her mother. Indeed, this seemed to go some way towards healing the pain.

Through the darkness, she became aware of light. It was pink, violet and blue sweeping across and around her. It swirled through her whole being and took away more and more of the cold darkness. Following the colours, she noticed that all around a brighter light was drawing her attention. She did not want to leave her mother but there was no doubt of the force of this all consuming power. A voice inside her head called out.

"It's all right Anna. It's all right to go. Look carefully, you will see someone who has come for you."

She obeyed the inner voice and looked into the light. Yes, faintly at first and then clearer, she saw her grandmother, smiling and reaching out to her, beckoning her to enter the brightness without fear or hesitation. Anna turned for one last time towards her mother, sending out a strong wave of love and then went into the light and took her grandmother's hand.

A DEADLY GAME

Tony felt the pain dig into his head and changed his mind. He disappeared under the pillow in an attempt to block out the daylight. After a night in a dry city, he had the mother of all hangovers and as his memory flooded back, he realised that he was lighter in pocket as a result of the last night's game. Welcome oblivion returned for an hour or so, after which he tried to surface again. *A Prairie Oyster and a walk in the park should do it*, he thought, opening both eyes and reaching for his watch. He struggled out of bed, threw some water over his face and looked in the mirror. He ran his fingers over the stubble and decided there was no need for a shave.

The sidewalk was busy and the police drove by. He pulled his collar up, kept his head down and made for the park. He could walk through, clear his brain and get to Benny's on 57th for some strong coffee and a cigarette. A spell in the green part of the city was just what the doctor ordered and he started to feel better. Benny's was busy and noisy as usual but you could almost stand a spoon in the coffee and the nicotine was kicking in. Benny himself was stuck in an exchange with a suit from the 'Street' (he had investments) but he nodded towards Tony and made his way over when the suit returned to the 'Journal.'

"Ciao Tony. Joe was in here looking for you. Said if I saw you to tell you to stop by, capice?"

Tony did understand. There was no hope of ignoring a message from Joe and no chance of passing the time of day with idle conversation if he'd been summoned.

"Sure, Benny, thanks. Arrivederci." He drained his cup, took a long drag of his cigarette and headed back out onto the city streets. Joe's message could only mean trouble and he'd thought the day was getting better. How mistaken he was.

He turned into 7th Avenue, past Carnegie Hall and took a left onto 49th. Joe's was not far from St. Patrick's and it was even said that the man himself went to Mass there. *They could employ a full-time priest to hear his confessions*, thought Tony and then decided that he wasn't qualified to sit in judgement on his associate.

The small door was locked but a couple of taps brought a response. Tony was recognised and allowed up the stairs. It took a while to get his eyes accustomed to the light (or rather lack of it) in the room. Eventually he realised that Joe was at a table at the back staring into a black coffee.

"Ciao, Tony, good to see you. Pull up a chair so we can talk."

Tony sat down accepting the offer of more coffee. He needed to think...fast.

"Truth is Tony, I've got a problem and I remembered you owed me a favour, after that time I took care of Big Pat. You've always struck me as the sort of guy who pays his debts."

Tony pulled in the smoke and exhaled, giving himself time.

"Sure, Joe, what gives?"

"It's last night's game. I lost; it was rigged. I don't like to lose. Word is Capone's boys are looking to set up in the 'Apple.' Checking out the competition, Freddie the Fire decided to try his hand at our little game without getting his fingers burned. I want him taken out Tony. No fuss, but I want Capone to know why. We've got to warn them off our patch and we can't be seen to roll over so easy. You've got talent; you could do it. I'll get a couple of the boys to go with you, to help you out."

Tony stubbed out his cigarette hard and drained the coffee cup. What a day this was turning out to be. Just what he needed, a tangle with Capone and minders along, just to make sure he didn't chicken out. Of course, Joe knew Tony was against the wall.

"Well, what d'y'a think?"

Tony took the cigarette offered to him and the light. Not quite the last smoke of the condemned man, but time was running through that hour glass and he had to admit, bright ideas eluded him.

"Know where these hoods can be found?"

He knew the answer. Joe was thorough. Nothing left to chance. He'd even asked Tony (who was expendable).

Joe just nodded. "Leave it to me, son. Just be outside O'Neill's at 11pm tonight. The boys'll pick you up. I'll even provide the shooter and they'll dispose of it when the job's done. There'll be an alibi of course but it would be a good idea if you'd lie low for a while afterwards. You might think of taking a vacation. The Cape's restful this time of year, so I'm told."

Tony doubted that he'd need an alibi or a vacation but he knew that if he survived, he'd have to get away. Capone's organisation was slick and in New York, talk was cheap.

He left Joe's and headed back towards the Park. What could he do with the last hours of his life? He wondered why it was such a sunny day when he was feeling so bad. He thought of going to see Annie but she'd bawled him out days ago. She'd talk sense and he didn't want to hear it. His sense said sort things out; money, a gun, a few things for a quick get away. Perhaps he'd call Annie, apologise and tell her he'd be going out of town for a while but he'd call her again when he got back.

10-55pm. Tony was outside O'Neill's and breaking into a sweat. He was almost changing his mind when the hired help arrived and he realised there was no way out. Natural to have a few mad minutes dreaming of escape but the reality was Joe or Capone? In New York, Joe won hands down, so he'd just have to get on with it. A short ride across town towards the Hudson led to a door at the side of a laundry. Joe's boys had done their homework and with the right knock on the door, they were in. The doorman must've been in on the act because he stood aside and they charged straight upstairs. They burst into the room and as ordered, Tony sprayed gunfire at the group of men huddled around a card game. His main aim was at the red-haired Freddie, who hardly registered surprise when the bullets pierced an ace and then his chest. As the rest reached for their guns, Tony knew he could not leave any alive. His eyes darted around the scene of carnage and then he turned towards the door.

The pain was sharp and intense. He flinched but it was gone in an instant. The red mist in front of him was from the blood-spattered mirror and his blurring eyes. The pain was in his back, just below the shoulder blade. The gun fell from his hands and he felt himself slump forwards, aware of the floor as he crashed onto it. He lay there twitching, blood spluttering from his mouth. He felt his fingers which had been clenched in pain roughly prised open so that the dropped gun could be stuck into his hand. He was powerless to resist; every fibre of his being concentrating on the act of dying. His last breath choked out without ceremony as Joe's boys went through his pockets and relieved him of every dime. What did a corpse want with money after all?

Tony stood up but the gun didn't come with him; if it had, he'd have taken out the hired help. He saw them look behind the bar, find some hooch and pour themselves two large glasses. Killing was thirsty work! He was right by them and aimed a punch just before Pat's glass touched his lips. Tony's fist went through Pat's face and the drink was drained and slammed back on to the bar. Tony swore in frustration; he could only watch these goons and he felt eaten away with anger. As the 'help' went through the pockets of the dead taking their payoff, Tony wrestled with rage. It tore through his ghost like the bullets that had felled him. The room grew dim and hazy; he felt a cold darkness he hadn't noticed before. He gradually became aware of the others, the gamblers, who had played their last game. They had been taken out, betrayed even as the cards hit the table. He could sense their anger and despair in death mixed with the frustration that they were powerless to inflict revenge upon their attackers. The 'help' stuffed piles of dollars into their jackets, spoils that Joe was unlikely to have sanctioned. Were they too stupid or too greedy to see how it all looked?

The Feds were no fools; a corpse with a gun would have still been in possession of the money, if he had taken it. Despite their clumsy attempts at wiping prints, it wouldn't be long before New York's finest would be knocking on Joe's door, having put his name in the frame.

The 'help' didn't seem in much of a rush. Having located the booze, they continued to enjoy it, surveying the scene through bleary eyes with some satisfaction. Tony wasn't the only ghost to be drawn towards them with thoughts of revenge.

"You've sure been stitched up by these slimeballs," observed Freddie -the -Fire. "Big Al's no idiot, he'll be sending Joe something in return. This is just a minor war. He's got plenty going in Chicago."

Tony agreed. "I knew it was a set up but I hoped I'd get away. Should've figured on the bullet in the back; bit slow today, heavy night last night. That's the problem with Prohibition, there's too much booze around; just can't avoid it."

Freddie's ghost saw the joke and laughed. They were starting to get used to being dead.

"No hard feelings. You were doing a job and at least you didn't shoot me in the back."

Tony felt a surprising warmth towards his victim and noticed a glow of light surrounding them both.

I'm sorry Freddie. You know the score but I won't take the wrap. The Feds'll be looking for Joe, 'specially when they get the doorman who let us in without a fuss."

Freddie looked surprised, "Ben? I thought he could be trusted. I'm sad to hear that. Now I know for certain, the only loyalty is to old Abraham Lincoln there."

A hollow empty laugh came from his shade, as he gestured towards the pile of dollar bills on the bar. Tony nodded.

"That's been my experience. Greed or fear (sometimes both), pull the strings in the 'city that never sleeps.' Guess it's probably the same in Chicago."

This time it was Freddie's turn to nod his agreement. His mind, still active, was trying to find a way to redress the balance in the deadly game.

"Hey Tony, come with me. Let's see if we can have some fun."

He moved towards the bar and reached for the glass which had been put down by one of 'the help.' His hand went right through it and he pulled back in annoyance. Tony went to the other 'help' and tried the same but it was as if he didn't exist. After several attempts clutching at air, Freddie concentrated hard in frustration. He wanted to move the glass with every atom of his non-being. His whole mind willed it to move and this time it did. The glass sped across the bar onto the floor with a crash. Seconds later, Tony achieved the same result with the other glass and the pile of dollar bills rose high in the air, as if a gust of wind had blown them around the room. One of the 'help' flailed about in panic, grabbing at dollar bills as if in a race against time. The other one shook from head to toe, his face so white, he could have joined the dead.

"What're you doing? I'm getting out of here," he yelled, making for the door which slammed shut. His friend continued his frantic attempts to catch the money which swirled about the room like snowflakes caught in a blizzard. He gasped as he called out,

"Go if you like. I'm getting the money. They're not spooking me."

At this point, the gun pulled itself out of Tony's fingers and turned towards the one who was heading for the door. He threw himself at the handle and wrenched it open, bullets flying all around him. This was enough to divert the other away from the money and he too launched himself across the room, wildly pushing tables and chairs aside in his panic. He hurtled through the open door, falling down the stairs on top of his friend as the bullets ricocheted from wall to wall and step to step. By this time there were a lot of happy ghosts around the speakeasy. Eventually, 'the help' picked themselves off the floor and stumbled onto the sidewalk dazed and trembling. They had been taught a lesson 'in style'. The souls of the departed had had their fun with the acquiescence of the universe and had forged a new found camaraderie in the process.

When the laughs died down, they looked around with uncertainty. For a while no-one spoke, then Tony's words burst through the silence.

"What happens now? I don't fancy being a ghost in a haunted speakeasy. Talk about Prohibition, we wouldn't have any booze!"

Freddie's thoughts echoed those of the other gamblers.

"Don't know about the hereafter. I've killed, lied, cheated at cards and thieved my way through life. Even then, I don't reckon I'm as bad as the low life we chased outa here."

The assembled company agreed, but all of them felt anxious about the prospect of an afterlife. Thoughts of the past pulled them all into darkness which collected around them and they felt the cold pain that they'd caused others. The room was filled with regret; sadness hung in the air like a mist but somewhere far off, compassion and understanding flooded through the icy fear and doubt. The life stories rolling by like silent films showed damaged children: no-hopers. The universe could accept the path taken by these souls who would be given the opportunity to make amends in the future.

Gradually, a clearing could be sensed in the gloom. Bright light seeped through the darkness. Tony's eyes were dazzled by the light. He wanted to shield his eyes, even though he had no physical body. He turned to Freddie,

"I guess that's the way to go. If we've got the guts to take it."

Freddie pulled away with trepidation as years of crime consumed his mind. The darkness engulfed him again but he had always been a fighter, prepared to take on the world. His mother had gone to her own death insisting that he had been born fighting! He forced himself through the misty thickness of despair towards Tony.

"I'll take my chances. Don't think there's much option. It can't be worse than that." He motioned towards the darkness that threatened to consume him with cold fear. Tony knew that he was right and was quick to agree.

"If I had to lay bets, I know which one would be odds on for Hell, so I'm for the light. Before I do, I just want to say sorry, no hard feelings?" He grinned at Freddie and the others, turned up his collar and walked into the whiteness as casually as if he was strolling along in Central Park.

Freddie laughed, surprised at the ease with which he could forgive the man who had taken his life.

"Yeh, brother, even the best families fight. We're in this together and we ain't been calling the shots."

Tony tipped his hat, understanding exactly what Freddie meant. Like foot soldiers in a war, they fought other people's battles, living and dying for someone else's gain. Freddie looked round at the other gamblers who had been aware of the conversation with his assassin.

"Sure, what does it matter? Forgiveness doesn't cost a dime and I think it's a start. It might just put me on the right path, who knows?

With this, he followed his old enemy and new found friend into the future.

GOOD LUCK CHARM

The sky darkened as the night closed in. Andy sprang into the cockpit and looked across the airfield at the others doing the same. With a minimum of fuss, the boys prepared for another dangerous night defending 'dear old Blighty'. Andy had just got back from a few dramatic days in London with Angie. Any time spent with Angie was full of incident. She lived life in a fast and furious style, which had become even more frantic during the war years. *Make the most of every moment,* she insisted. Live life to the full while you still have *a life to live! You're a long time dead,* seemed to be her excuse for everything. Days and nights merged together in a haze of champagne bubbles, West End shows and dancing at 'The Ritz'. Of course, he wasn't complaining. Grabbing every moment, meant nights of passion, intense erotic pleasures of the flesh; after all, a war was no time to save oneself!

Andy was plagued by the thought that Angie might apply this philosophy to all the men she met. Perhaps being faithful had no place in wartime either! He tried hard to block this from his mind and he would not discuss it with her; he did not want empty reassurances that he would probably doubt anyway. It was much better not to think about it, however hard that was. Of course their stolen moments were brief and bittersweet. One week off in six wasn't much to base a relationship on. Leaving was difficult and he often wondered if her defence was not to get too involved, especially with a flyer. Flyers lived on borrowed time; the more missions they flew, the less likely they were to return. He had flown nineteen and was just about to start his twentieth.

The boys were great, they were a terrific team and looked out for each other. Reggie was his navigator and Ben his gunner. They had to have sharp eyes and their wits about them; one slip and their war was over.

Andy's hand brushed his pocket and he remembered the small brown paper bag Angie had given him after the night before. He had laughed when he opened it; it was a small fluffy, grey rabbit.

"He's called 'Dizzy', like me. I know you think I'm dizzy, the way I run about all over the place, doing this and that. Take him with you for luck, please."

He had tucked Dizzy down into his uniform pocket, feeling that he was a bit of Angie flying with him that night. He patted his pocket,

'Well Dizzy, here we go. Hope you like flying. Up, up and away, Bun!'

He signalled to the crew that he was ready for take off and the Bristol Blenheim soon gathered speed as it prepared for lift off. Andy felt the thrill as much as ever, combined with that nervous, sick feeling in the pit of his stomach. It didn't matter, it was soon over and the adrenaline kicked in hard. No more thoughts of death; he was very much alive and he had a job to do. He had told himself often that the nerves were a good thing, a self preservation making him take extra care. Certainly, no-one could accuse him of LMF(lack of moral fibre). So many nights they'd sat around playing cards, waiting for the others to return, counting them in, one at a time. He knew the sound of each engine and any splutter out of place would tell him if there was a problem. Often, it was ok; all the planes came back: but not always. He'd lost good friends and it didn't get any easier. Knowing you could be next couldn't be avoided; that was how it was. The more runs you did, the more likely you'd be

'gone for a Burton'. The betting odds were poor and for him they were shortening. He looked at the good luck rabbit and wondered if charms could lengthen the odds.

It was a special night, the Luftwaffe had been carrying out increased raids on Britain. The industrial cities had had the worst of it: London, Liverpool, Coventry: places he had known well before the war. Now there were so many bombed out areas and the dark blacked out nights made them morbid and depressing. Only the people, who retained their humour made them bearable. The British were determined to put a brave face on it; they would not let the war get the better of them, no matter what happened. It was the spirit embodied by Winston and that was why he was such a great leader.

Andy hoped that if they stepped up the raids, it would help to end the war and give victory to the allies. Flying was great but he'd started to wonder what it would be like piloting a plane in peacetime; would he even get to find out? His thoughts were interrupted by Reggie who was in good humour as usual.

"Hey, I don't know about the extra passenger," he said with a nod towards the grey rabbit.

"That's Dizzy. He's a good luck charm."

Reggie just laughed,

"Another one? Soon be no room for us!" Reggie set his eyes on the night sky.

Andy lifted the rabbit down carefully.

"Don't worry, Diz. He doesn't mean it. You're welcome aboard, but it could be a rough ride this time, so you'd better hold on tight!" He gave the rabbit a reassuring pat on the head.

They flew over the Kent countryside and on to the Channel. It seemed strangely quiet but they knew from experience that it was unlikely to last. Reggie was thoughtful for once.

"You serious?"

"About the rabbit? Of course. He'll bring us luck tonight; I'm sure of it."

"About Angie?"

Andy sighed. "Would be, if she'd have me. You never know with Angie. She always says she's free as a bird. Still, I've decided to find out. Next leave I go on, I'll pop the question; take the bull by the horns so to speak."

Reggie laughed.

"We've got rabbits, birds and now bulls; but good luck old chap. She's a looker and no mistake."

They were nearing the Belgian coast, when they heard the familiar sound of a nearby plane. Andy called back to Ben,

"Can you see it? Near enough to have a shot?"

Ben had found it and tried to get it in his sights.

"It's at 5 o'clock." Almost as soon as he answered, Ben attempted to take down their pursuer. Andy tried to manoeuvre the plane into a better position whilst trying to avoid the enemy fire. The sound of the air fight seemed magnified inside the tiny cockpit and the plane started to struggle.

"Got him!" shouted Ben, just as Andy was almost giving up hope of success.

The German plane sped blazing towards the cold depths of the sea; that particular battle was over. Relief, however was short-lived.

"We're losing height; we've been hit!" Reggie confirmed what Andy had suspected.

"Just steady her and we'll look for somewhere to land."

Andy managed to gain some control, although he knew they would have to bring the plane down; there was no hope of getting back home.

"The load?" Reggie asked but already knew the answer.

"We'll have to jettison before we land. It had better be soon." In his head, Andy ran through his knowledge of the landscape. They needed to avoid towns so that they didn't take innocent Belgian lives. Was there any chance of hitting an enemy camp?

"There's woodland ahead. It'll have to do. We can't guarantee getting much further, especially full weight."

The bombs were dropped, exploding in a flash of light, just high enough to get away, but it was a close call. They picked up a little height and flew on, hoping to find somewhere equally remote to land safely.

Having to fly much closer to the ground, they were riding their luck and Andy knew it; time was running out. He thought he could see a clearing ahead and prepared to land, offering up a silent prayer. As they approached, the sound of gunfire could be heard, with sparks of stuttering light spraying out towards them. Flak peppered into the fusillade and the plane dived, the ground rushing up to meet it. There was no time for the crew to bail out. Andy braced himself for impact but called out,

"That's it lads. Good luck!"

He knew that it was unlikely they would survive the crash and deep inside, a little voice told him it might be better that way. Thoughts flashed by in an instant and his mind filled with Angie."

"So sorry, Angie," he murmured as the twisted metal of the bomber hit the ground and everything went black around him.

Hans Durer had been having a smoke, when he realised that his men had brought down an enemy plane. He threw the cigarette into a muddy puddle and ran to investigate.

Ordering two of the men to accompany him, he made his way across the fields. They approached the wreckage cautiously, guns ready to deal with survivors. It was hard to tell if there were bodies inside the cockpit which was mangled beyond recognition and the rest of the plane was scattered over a considerable area. It would take time to check it.

Andy was in a dream, floating over fields of darkness. He couldn't remember anything. What had happened? If he was asleep, it felt strange; he must be in that just waking state, when dreams are vivid and seem like reality and yet at the same time, you know something's not quite right. As he became aware of the debris which had been his plane, he started to recall the circumstances of the crash. He noticed the German soldiers sifting through the metal and searching the ground around the plane. One of the soldiers had wandered off towards a tree. He turned and shouted to the others.

"Quick, quick, an airman."

Two others ran up, guns in their hands.

"He must be dead, is he not?" The man who appeared to be in charge asked the soldier who had called them over.

As if in reply, the body on the ground let out a groan of pain.

"We should take him prisoner," said the soldier who had found the body.

One of the others disagreed. "He has lost a lot of blood. He won't survive and we can't look after him."

The man in charge looked at the gun in his hand and flicked off the safety catch.

"He might have information but I don't think he is in a condition to talk."

He pointed the gun and fired two shots into the wounded man's chest. Andy was desperate to know who the German had killed and found himself staring intently at the body which was still oozing blood; it was Reggie. Well at least the war was over for him and he was out of pain. He couldn't stop the wave of sorrow that washed over him as he took on the responsibility for the crash. Why couldn't he save these men who had trusted him so completely? When the pain of his actions swelled inside, he felt cold darkness surrounding him, which pressed from every side. Despite his sadness, he couldn't cry; the tears would not come. He turned away, still overcome by the pain.

The Germans were still examining the wreckage, carefully looking for anything significant. Andy noticed a figure a little way off, staring at the scattered fuselage. The shape drifted, appearing dazed; it was Reggie; but of course, that was impossible; he was lying on the ground splattered with blood and bullets. Reggie was dead and this figure was his ghost. Andy surveyed the scene of devastation and reality kicked him hard. As it did so, he noticed a grey ball of fluff with an ear sticking out. A bloodstained Dizzy had been tossed across the field and lay amid the wreckage. His thoughts turned to Angie and the agony that he would never see her again was unbearable. Some good luck charm that rabbit turned out to be! Stupid as it seemed, he couldn't help worrying how she'd feel, knowing that he must have taken her last gift with him on the fateful mission. He wanted to sink into the ground and cry but again the emotion welled up within him like a hard ball of cold pain. He knew she would grieve for him but hopefully not for long. She would find someone to comfort her and in her fast life it would be easier to move on. He hoped she would remember the good times: even fleetingly.

He had to put the emotion of parting behind him, however difficult. His training was slowly recalled and he knew that he had to look after his crew. He could see Reggie, but where was Ben? Surely he couldn't have survived? Anyway, the Germans would have finished him off, just as they had Reggie; he was sure of that. With these thoughts racing through his mind, he looked up to meet Reggie's eyes.

Reggie looked so relieved,

"How've we got out of that? The last thing I remember was coming in too fast over the trees; there was a noise and everything went black. I must have been thrown clear but when I started to come round, I heard voices. I was in so much pain: I think I was drifting in and out of consciousness. I tried to make out what the voices were saying but it seemed so far away. All I could think about was the pain. I tried to speak but it wouldn't come out. There was a noise like an explosion and the pain flared and then stopped so suddenly I couldn't believe it. I was standing in the field looking at ...this." He turned to the bits of plane strewn across the grass.

Andy couldn't find a way to break it gently.

"We're dead, Reggie. That's it; it's all over for us: everything."

"What do you mean dead?" Reggie spoke slowly, as if he was trying to process the information.

"The Germans shot you. They talked about it for a bit and decided that you were too injured to take prisoner."

The sudden sight of his own body helped Reggie to understand and everything fell into place. He looked around, wondering where the Germans were.

"What about Ben?"

Andy scanned the wreckage, desperately trying to find the young gunner. As light blazed around them, he could see Ben walking purposefully forward. He stopped, turned and looked across at them with a nod. Focused once more, he continued and they knew what to do; they moved to join him. Andy was drawn to the grey rabbit once again and thought how stupid it was that he wanted to take a failed good luck charm into the afterlife. Maybe he just didn't want to leave it in Germany.

You just can't do it, he thought to himself. *They always say there are no pockets in a shroud!* As he looked at Dizzy, he could see Angie laughing, a glass of Champagne in her hand. She shivered and her eyes betrayed a stray thought of him. She shook her blonde curls as if to wake herself up, sipped her drink and then focused once more on her friends. Andy knew he must do the same. He pulled himself away from the mindset which kept him earthbound and looked to the future: his future.

The wreckage of the plane started to fade into the night mist and a powerful light could be seen behind the silhouetted trees. The light moved closer so that the trees seemed to disappear.

"Well, Lads, it's got to be that way, I reckon. That light's got to be the way to go now. Let's get out of this war. We've done our bit. What's next?"

The others nodded. There could be no argument and after all, he was still their leader. They went forward together into the blinding light and knew that they had found their peace.

THE GRIM REAPER

The house was always welcoming. It rang with music and laughter, family dinners, parties and conversation with friends long into the night (setting the world to rights, they often said). Deep, philosophical discussion took place, examining the meaning of life. All were invited into this hospitable home.

Today, there was an unfamiliar guest. Death waited, knowing he would soon be able to claim his property. It was time. But even he tiptoed cautiously around the gloom, so out of place, struggling to invade the atmosphere of peaceful calm. Indeed, the family moved quietly through the rooms, all too aware of Death's brooding presence in their home. Yet the soul for whom this grim reaper waited was content, having lived a full life, to pass through the doors to eternity. The reason for this peaceful acceptance could be summed up in a single word: faith.

The woman of advanced years lying in the main bedroom upstairs had led, not a blameless life, but one that had been lived to the glory of Jesus Christ. His life and example had provided a beacon for her chosen path. When she had strayed, he had taken her hand and guided her back to his way because he knew what was within her heart. She, in turn, would ask forgiveness for the times when she had just not got it right and would pray for his help in the future. Now, at the doorway into another world, she had regrets but she knew that she had tried to follow God's Son and she believed that before many days had passed, she would see him in his glory and be with him in Heaven.

For some time, Hope (for that was her name) had been more and more detached from life. She drifted in and out of sleep, unaware of night and day. She enquired about news in rare conversation, out of politeness and her own kindly concern for others, rather than any real interest in the world of which she was still a part: for now. She had voted in the recent General Election with the usual sense of responsibility, although she knew that the incoming government could have little impact upon her future.

Hope had no wish to leave her loved ones; it would be hard to say those final goodbyes which she felt strongly must be said very soon. It would be a wrench to pull herself away from them and everything that was so familiar to her, but then she knew that she would soon be reunited with other loved ones who had gone before her, taking that leap into the unknown at the close of their lives. Indeed, sad parting would give way to happy reunion (or so she believed) and at her time of life, there were many happy reunions to look forward to, as so many of those close to her had passed away. Hope felt sure that she had met some of them in her dreams; they walked by the sea or along the banks of flowing rivers where fresh flowers filled the breeze with their scent. When she woke, it was often with disappointment, wanting her dreams to be never-ending, rather than return to the harsh reality of pain and discomfort. Her waking moments were becoming increasingly difficult; shortness of breath, a dull ache and sharper pain were evident when the heavy medication wore off.

One evening, Hope opened her eyes and looked around the familiar room. From her bed, she could see through the window, albeit in the haze of poor, drugged sight. Surprisingly, the view looked clearer than it had for some time: a deep, glorious sunset. Earth's beauty was captured in timeless tranquility. How she used to love the marvellous sunsets that were a feature of her home. She gazed upon it until the sun died in the sky and wondered if it would be for the last time. She became aware that she could not feel the pain she had become so accustomed to.

I feel so much better, she thought. *Perhaps I'm not going anywhere. I may recover after all. What a complete fraud I have been!*

The Grim Reaper smiled a knowing smile; everything was going well. He withdrew a little, satisfied just to wait.

After a time, realisation dawned. Of course, it was the usual improvement before the final decline. How many times had she observed it in others? How often had she been the concerned and grieving relative, sitting out those last, difficult days? *It's time to say goodbye,* she decided. *I must not lose this chance, there will not be another.*

The door of the bedroom opened and her daughter Ruth came in carrying a tray with soup and medicine.

"You've been so much better today, Mum. Perhaps tomorrow we could…" She paused, sensing that her words were out of place.

The patient responded, "Thank you so much, Ruth ."

"Whatever for?"

Her daughter took her hand.

"For helping me to stay here."

"It's your home, Mum. It's where you should be."

The old lady smiled weakly and sighed. She couldn't manage all the words she wished to say. It was too much effort to speak.

"Andrew? George? Vicky? I want to see them."

The close understanding between them made further explanations unnecessary.

Arrangements were made and the loving family gathered around the bedside with a deep sadness which they tried hard not to show. There would be time for grieving but for these precious hours, the main thing was to be positive and to listen to the woman whose life was ebbing away before their eyes.

Her voice was almost a frail whisper as she spoke, "Thank you for all the happy times and for all your love. No-one could have a better family. I love you all; I always will."

They murmured their love with tear-filled eyes, trying desperately to control their emotion. The woman smiled, although weak, she was content. She had told them of her love and that was of great importance to her. However, there was one more thing that she knew must be said.

"I have planned my funeral: look in the top drawer of the bureau. I want it to be a celebration of a very happy life. I've been so lucky and I am going home. This journey is at an end but another one is beginning. I will be there for all of you when your time comes. We will meet again."

She knew how lucky she was to have been able to speak to her family. To have passed on her message of love. There was one more thing she wanted to do.

"Can we all pray together?" Hope struggled to reach for the olive wood cross she had kept by her bedside for years since a visit to Jerusalem. She had always found comfort when she held it but this time her fingers could not reach it. Her daughter placed it in her hand, softly closing her fingers over it, noticing the sense of relief it brought.

The onlookers fought back their tears to join in a family prayer, thanking God for the gentle soul and for the special joy which she had brought into the lives of each of them. They followed with the Lord's Prayer and a sense of calm filled the room as never before. The woman sank a little deeper into her pillows, resting with a serene contentment.

Now, she could face the end. She had done everything necessary to meet her maker in peace.

Although the end did not come that night, her condition started to deteriorate more rapidly. Death drew a little closer to the room and then entered quietly but stayed in the shadows. The family kept a vigil by the bedside, making sure someone was always there.

Hope's words became fewer, until she no longer spoke. She was fading gradually but they could still hold her hand and listen carefully for the breathing that told them she was still of this world, aware that she was becoming weaker and her breathing barely audible. Sometimes, the gentle pressure of her hand or a faint smile, told them that she knew of their presence. This was her only communication as she drifted further away and the family knew that the hour of her death was very near. For her part, she was embracing death, knowing she could find no way back into the material world. The pain and life itself had been virtually obliterated by the drugs she had taken; people around her were shadowy presences drifting further away from her consciousness. Finally but quietly she crossed the divide, a sigh marking her final moment. Death had claimed another soul and was content.

Floating high in the room, she became aware of the shadowy bed surrounded by quietly weeping figures. The emotion of the scene pulled her down towards them but they were unaware of her. She felt frustrated by their inability to notice her, especially because she was experiencing such an overwhelming sense of freedom from the pain that had itself seemed eternal. Their grief was mirrored in her emotions and a wave of pity swept across her soul while she hovered near to them. Their tears seemed worse because she survived as she had known she would and she was now released from the burden that had been her body. She had tried to tell them not to mourn, all to no avail. Death had triumphed within the house where the good soul's serenity had ruled for an age. Now, Death in all its misery was content to feed upon the empty desolation that the family felt because she had left them. Quietly, they left the room, to make the arrangements necessary at such times.

The departed soul contemplated the frail body that she had occupied for so long, but could not feel a connection to it; it was like a stranger, lying there as if a waxwork.

Why didn't she feel sorrow or at least something for her earthly self? She couldn't answer the question but her lack of feeling was in itself powerful. If anything, it was like being released from a prison; certainly that was what it had felt like for some time through her long illness. No, she couldn't identify with this body ravaged by time. She was young again and more than that, she was different: complete. She had begun to rediscover something from within; long forgotten but precious: a part of her very soul that had remained out of reach to her while she had inhabited an earthly body. These thoughts flashed through her mind: powerful impressions moving through her spirit consciousness at an amazing speed. The events of her life flashed before her like a film. Although she was an observer, she could feel the emotions felt by others and generated by her own actions. At times, she felt the pain that she had inflicted on others, often without realising. Her shade was filled with sadness and compassion for those she had hurt and she was desperate to make amends and receive forgiveness. Her heart filled with love and a new understanding. Perhaps in death, life's lessons could still be learned and it was not too late, even though the damage had been done. The warmth of love fought to drive out the coldness of pain and regret brought indeed by the Grim Reaper. It was a confusing mixture of feeling, too complex to truly understand but she was able to work through it and move away from the dark pain.

She rose towards the side of the room, without thinking about what she was doing. Light streamed through the window even though it was night and thus dark outside. The beam of light appeared to be coming from the heavens; like a stairway. Her gaze became transfixed upon this and she began to see figures descending the beam. They reached out to her, just as they had in her dreams, but this time, she knew that she could go with them and she would not return to the sick body she had abandoned. As she recognised them, she felt a deep warmth flood through her ethereal being. She knew that her husband and her family members who had long passed on were there to be reunited and to guide her on her journey. They were smiling and welcoming her, filling her heart with joy so that she felt she would almost burst with happiness. No sadness here, only delight at a homecoming, everything was as it should be.

She took one last look at the room and the body lying on the bed as its final pull tried to claim her soul with its earthbound strength but that was not to be. It was the natural order of things and it was her time to move on. She had said her goodbyes and there was little more that she could do there. Her mind had worked through the grief at parting from her living family for so many months and the more recent days of her illness and she knew that nothing could be done. She had to embrace death and move on to continue her own journey.

Her husband and parents moved forward. Surrounding her, they took her hands and led her up along the beam of light. It was effortless and she trusted them completely. A tunnel opened in front of them bathed in light and they continued, travelling easily through, ignoring any diversions from their chosen path. Sometimes, she thought she heard faint voices calling through the tunnel but she knew they were unimportant: for her. The journey had a vague familiarity and yet she could not explain why. It was enough to be guided and to know all was right.

Nearing the end of the tunnel, they approached a heavy door, but passed through it without hindrance. They were in a garden and could hear the most beautiful birdsong. The colours of the flowers were vibrant and the grass, greener than she could ever remember.

A plant-covered wall surrounded one part of the garden, leading to a low fountain near a stone seat. The woman's eyes were drawn towards this as she noticed a man in white who was sitting there. He looked up and beckoned to her. Her companions nodded and she went with them. She knew of course, his identity and was filled with awe and amazement that he would be there for such a lowly soul. As she gazed deep into his eyes, into eternity, she knew how wrong such feelings were. He was there for anyone who looked for him and now she had no doubt that this was her journey's end.

In the house, filled with mourning, the Grim Reaper smiled a cold, satisfied smile. It was done but it was a shallow satisfaction. This death was not a great triumph: at least, not for him.

THE TUNNEL

Sandy crept down to her usual place in the tunnel and pulled the old duvet over her head.

Why did she come here? They didn't want her, unless she had glue. Tonight they'd been pleased to see her, so friendly, falling over themselves to share her stuff. At least they had, until she had argued with that girl, the one with purple hair. Who did she think she was? Just because she used to sing with that group (the one packing the punters in at the club down the road), till they dumped her when the drugs took over.

Now, they were just the same, two worthless junkies: glue heads, off their faces and right off the planet. No-one cared, no-one bothered to look down the tunnel at night, where the discarded remnants, the rubbish of society managed to forget who they were and why they existed.

Sandy felt sick and wondered if she would throw up. It didn't matter, she was used to it. She'd just turn her head, throw up and then maybe sink into sleep. She looked into the dark with bleary eyes, everything swimming in front of her. The fire they'd made was dying down but the red embers flared up like monsters riding towards her, flaming tendrils stretched out threatening to engulf her in flames. No, she closed her eyes and turned away, hiding once again in the duvet before the urge to be sick made her lurch to one side and slump against the wall. Sinking into sleep, she avoided the angry taunts of the purple-haired girl who seemed to want their fight to carry on. The vomit rose in

Sandy's throat again, but she lay inert as it exploded inside her, choking her sleeping breath.

Sandy's spluttering convinced the purple-haired girl that the fight was on again. She forced herself to stagger along the tunnel to where Sandy lay and kicked hard at the feet sticking out of the battered duvet.

"Ger up an' fight, yer fat cow!" She screamed at Sandy, still kicking but getting no response.

"Yer can't fight me, can yer? She's useless, everyone. Ain't she useless?"

The girl turned to register the agreement of the others in the tunnel. They were not interested in the cat fight, commonplace among the group, so she turned back towards Sandy and after another forceful kick, decided to pull at the long red hair which was sticking out of the duvet. She leaned down to grasp the hair but lost her balance and landed on top of the duvet, collapsing in an unconscious heap.

Sandy found herself wandering through the darkness of the tunnel looking at a bright light shining up ahead. The glue still exercised its control; her head swam with confusion. She started to walk towards the light, then stopped, suspicious as always of the light of day and the truth that it would reveal about her. She turned round and noticed figures in the dark. The others haven't gone, she thought. I'm not on my own. She moved towards them but they were moving away and she couldn't seem to reach them.

"Don't go without me," she shouted out.

They took no notice. A little way ahead, she saw the purple-haired girl and her heart sank. The girl had just noticed Sandy and looked as though she still wanted a fight.

Why can't she just leave it out? I'm not interested. Sandy thought and wondered if it would be better to go towards the light. At least then, she wouldn't have to fight. After all if they were both in the light, people would see how the fights started and maybe someone would actually bother to stop them.

Suddenly, the girl was there, right beside her. She seemed as surprised as Sandy but it didn't stop her quick reaction as she scratched her long fingernails into Sandy's face. There was no time for Sandy to stop the scratch and she felt for the blood as she delivered a kick and then tried to grab the purple hair. She could not pull on the hair and there was no blood on her hands. What was going on? The girl seemed as confused as she was, still trying to draw blood in any way she could but without success. Their fight had taken them back along the tunnel a little and they became aware of voices. There was a group ahead clustered around something on the ground. The girls stopped the fight (which was getting nowhere) as their attention was attracted by the commotion. They approached the group and Sandy called out to a boy at the edge.

"Hey, Skate, what's goin' on?"

He ignored her and fixed his eyes on something on the floor. It was hard to see anything and then Sandy noticed a shock of purple hair sticking out over the boy's boot. His foot moved and she saw the white hand with long black nails (the same ones that had just tried so hard to scratch her face) but they lay motionless. She turned to the girl.

"Look's like you, funny that."

"It is me," interrupted the girl, "and you."

"What d'ya mean?"

Sandy pushed the boy, trying to get a better look but he didn't move and didn't even turn on her with anger as she expected.

"I mean we're dead, both of us. That's me, an you're under the duvet. I didn't kill yer though; you were dead before I fell on yer. Choked on the glue, I reckon."

Sandy swung round to argue and then stopped. A gap appeared in the group as someone walked away and she forced herself to look down at the crumpled duvet and saw her own face, sightless eyes staring where they checked for signs of life.

"But we're here! WE'RE HERE!" She screamed at the group who were disappearing along the tunnel. She ran after them, determined to make them see her. She was real, why couldn't they see that? They just carried on walking, completely ignoring her.

"I'M NOT DEAD! YOU USELESS LOAD OF JUNKIES! CAN'T YOU HEAR ME?"

It was hopeless. Either they couldn't hear her, or they were pretending for a joke.

Yeh, that's it, she thought. *It's a wind up. They can hear me. They're all in on it.*

It was an idea, but not convincing. Deep down, she knew that someone would have turned round when she shouted, probably just to swear at her; they wouldn't have been able to resist it.

She tried not to think about the white face under the filthy duvet but it kept coming back to her and she forced herself to go back and look at it again. This time, without the crowd, she couldn't hide from the truth. It was clear; they were dead.

Later…

When the bodies had been removed and Sandy had given up trying to be noticed, she sat down in the tunnel much as usual with the purple-haired girl. They couldn't fight and didn't feel hungry but they crouched in the dark as they had often done, confused and lost in their isolation. They were silent but a torrent of thoughts bombarded them both as they wondered if anyone would actually miss them. Neither of them had much in the way of a home, but still there were people at the back of their minds if they searched hard. People who had become lost in the drugged haze that had become their brains.

"Me nan'll be asking for me. She's not well since she had that fall. She used to like it when I went round. We'd talk for hours; she told me what it was like when she was a girl, and what it was like in the war when Grandad was away fighting in the army. She listened to me; she didn't spend all the time shouting and moaning like me mum."

Sandy noticed the light again. She was drawn towards it as she thought of her nan and she felt warmer just as she had in her grandmother's house. The purple-haired girl seemed to understand,

"Yeh, my granny lived too far away for me to see her much, but it was great when I did. She was always fussing over me and giving me things. She made me dinners and we'd watch the telly."

She felt the wave of warmth and the light that Sandy had been drawn to.

"Hey, Sand," she paused, reluctant to speak her thoughts. Slowly, she asked the burning question. "Do you think we could go to Heaven?"

"Too late, too late, too late!"

Voices whispered from the darkness deep in the tunnel and shapes could be seen drifting towards them.

"Heaven doesn't want you . You were bad. Bad girls! You're gone. Lost: lost forever. Come with us. Hide in the dark. No-one can find you there. We like bad girls. Ha, ha, ha, ha."

The echoing laughter filled the tunnel till Sandy wanted to scream. She put her hands over her ears, but the noise pierced her whole being, the sound becoming part of her, vibrating through the shade that she had become. The coldness returned. They were right; it was too late. She was dead and her short life had been full of pain, despair and running away. In death she still ran, away from the light where she would have to face herself and God. What of God ?

Shame welled up inside her and she was pulled into the darkness.

"What did God ever do for you? You're like me. Why would God want us?"

The purple-haired girl sneered at the light which was shining at the other end of the tunnel and turned away from it, shielding her eyes. Sandy stared into the brightness and for a split second, she thought she saw the flash of an angel wing. She moved a little towards the light but stopped. Angels? She reconsidered. Daft! I'm imagining it. Why would God send angels for me? God wouldn't be interested in me. No, she decided, God would just be angry with her. Reading her mind, the voices continued.

"You'll pay. You'll have to pay, if you try to go to Heaven. They'll send you to Hell. You'll pay, you'll pay, you'll pay. It hurts, it hurts, the light burns you. Come away. Come away into the dark. You're safe there with us."

Their words hissed all around her until she didn't know if they were on the outside or if they were part of her very being. She was pulled into the pitch black with the purple-haired girl whose despair equalled her own.

The voices encircled them.

"You never bothered about God. Do you think he's going to bother about you now? Too late, too late. Hide, hide in the darkness in case they come looking for you."

"Who will come looking for us?" The purple-haired girl looked around in a panic.

"Redeemers, forces of light. Trying to get you; they'll make you answer for all the things you did. Bad girls, lots to answer for. We're like you. You can hide with us. We won't let them find you. Hide in the dark and find more bad things to do, ha, ha, ha, ha."

Sandy felt the cold darkness consume her. She looked at the purple-haired girl and felt that hope, which had sparked so briefly, had vanished. Their vacant eyes registered acceptance and they drifted further into the darkness of the tunnel to join the mocking voices of the abyss. The feeling was rather like the emptiness they were used to, but magnified so that every speck of hope was removed. They sensed the mocking pleasure of souls who had nothing positive to exist for and whose thin satisfaction depended on others joining them. The ghosts of the earthbound drifted towards the girls, coming to claim the prize of two more forlorn entities, fallen from the treadmill of eternity.

In her despair, Sandy thought again of her nan, knowing that the old lady really would mourn her loss. The sadness which engulfed her with the thought was of a different sort to the empty despair; it was warmer, fuelled by the moments shared with her grandmother over the years. Everything came rushing back to her, long forgotten times when she was young: laughter, tears and the ordinary everyday life that had disappeared with her descent into the world of drugs. Even her mother seemed to have cared for her in the past before they had been so forced apart. Her thoughts were selfless. She was filled with feelings of her mother and grandmother's loss, along with the knowledge that much of her mother's criticism had come from a caring love for her.

Sandy was filled with memories. Her soul was soothed by the love she could feel, even though this was mixed with an almost overwhelming sadness. Why had the realisation come so late, when she could do nothing to put things right?

She became aware of the light again and bravely determined to approach it. There was safety in numbers and she turned to reach out for the arm of the purple-haired girl, who though she could not hold on, understood Sandy's thoughts and drifted cautiously towards her. Together they moved forward.

"You'll hurt. It'll choke you and then, it'll burn you up. You'll see. Too late, too late." The voices continued their barrage of misery.

"We always get the junkies. You can't go there. You have to stay with us. You're used to the dark of the tunnel. Why change? Why change?"

But this time, it was different. This time, the voices knew they were losing. The girls continued their journey towards the light. The spark of love within them burned brighter with memories of every kindness they had ever received and even some that they had carried out. Long-lost in the drug- fogged recesses of their minds, the best moments of their lives surfaced, enfolding them in a glow of warmth which grew stronger and stronger as they drew closer.

The girls became more determined to fight the draw of the darkness which only strengthened with any chinks of self-doubt. In death, they found a strength for battle that they had lacked in their lifetime struggle with self- doubt, a suspicion of society and the lure of sniffing glue. They focused firmly on the light ahead, so that gradually, the voices behind them faded to a whisper until they could no longer be heard.

Sandy and the purple-haired girl continued to move towards the light. Becoming ever more confident in their decision, they were enfolded by its white brightness. They moved towards another tunnel which did not offer drugs and arguments, but healing love.

YOU'LL NEVER WALK ALONE

"We're going to Wem-ber-ley," they sang as they made the journey from Liverpool to Sheffield with scarves fluttering out of the car windows. Ed, Terry and Don, Southport Scousers looking forward to a day in the early April sun, watching their team win a place in the FA cup final.

"I fancy an all Merseyside final; reds and blues descending on Wembley, the Mersey invasion!" Ed stopped talking, to indicate and overtake another car full of fans on their way to the match.

"That'll do me," replied Terry. "I fancy us to beat the Toffees."

Don agreed. "King Kenny's men can beat anyone. I don't care who we get but a Merseyside final would be great. It'd be a bit quiet at work on Monday though, when we've been celebrating all weekend and 'the Bitters' have been drowning their sorrows."

The car gradually slowed and joined a long queue of traffic.

"Roadworks, typical! Good job we left early." Terry lit a cigarette and took a calming drag.

"Won't be early by the time we get through this," moaned Ed, turning on the car radio and trying to tune it to the sport. The car crept forward and ground to a halt again. Ed noticed a white envelope on the shelf under the dashboard.

"Oh, no! Can you remind me to post this card for our kid's birthday. Carol'll kill me if I go home with it."

Terry picked it up. "Here, put it in your pocket. We passed at least three boxes on the way out of town this morning but we're bound to see one on the way to the ground."

Ed managed to put the card in his pocket.

"Well, don't let me forget; she's a terror when she's mad. It's that fiery red hair and her father's Irish temper."

Don laughed. "They're all the same, mate, strike fear into any defence!"

Moving slowly, the car finally made it through the roadworks, but behind them there were cars as far as the eye could see.

Don looked back along the road.

"Looks like some people are going to miss kick off."

Terry groaned when he saw the line of cars behind them. "If they're lucky they'll make it, but they won't get a pint in before the game, that's for sure."

"Nor will we," laughed Ed. "Let's just make sure we get to the game in plenty of time. I don't want to be at the back of Leppings Lane."

Don agreed. "Yeh, I don't think we're going to be very early. Perhaps we can find a chippie though."

They drove into Sheffield, parked the car and set off to walk up the hill to Sheffield Wednesday's ground, where the game was taking place. Hillsborough was a strange little ground, hardly suitable for a cup semi-final, but they'd managed last year...(just). Its location was deemed accessible for both Liverpool and Nottingham Forest supporters, but spacious it was not.

Crowds were converging on the ground. They were in good humour, looking forward to an exciting afternoon of football. There weren't many turnstiles and it took a while to get through the increasing numbers of supporters.

Once inside, they were directed along a tunnel towards the Leppings Lane end, behind the goal where the Liverpool supporters were already forming a sea of red with the usual banners proclaiming the club's proud history. Liverpool FC had been founded in 1892 but had really grown to ascendancy under the guidance of the legendary Bill Shankly. Now the manager was Kenny Dalglish who had first come to the club as an amazing player. He was known as 'King Kenny' and immortalised in the famous song 'The Fields of Anfield Road.'

The terraces were filling up and as kick off approached, it promised to be a great day.

"Wonder if everyone'll get through the roadworks. I'd hate to miss this. It's fantastic weather as well." Don leaned against the barrier and surveyed the scene. "It feels like the whole of Liverpool's in the ground."

Terry looked round at the crowd.

"You're not wrong. When are they going to stop letting people in here? It's getting pretty squashed."

He sounded annoyed and Ed had to agree.

"Yeah, look at the Forest end. I'm sure there's more room and they don't seem to have as many fans."

Their mood was starting to be felt by others around them. Although they were no strangers to crowded terraces which swayed and moved as one, this was becoming more and more uncomfortable. Don could feel the barrier pressing into his stomach as people pushed forward.

"Make some space lads," a cry came from behind.

"There's no bloody space, you wazak," was the response from someone close by. "We're suffocating."

As the cheers rang out and the players ran onto the pitch, the problems on the terrace worsened. Supporters were still flooding onto Leppings Lane and yet those near the front were being pushed hard against the wire fence that caged them like animals. Terry was near the gate; he could see a bobby on the pitch and called out to him.

"Hey mate, it's too full in here, people are squashed. Can you get that gate open please?"

The policeman didn't even answer, but turned away.

"Open the fucking gate. People are dying in here," someone called out.

The crowd surged forward but there was nowhere to go. Hands reached down from the stands above, so that some people further back were able to be lifted out of the crush but not enough to ease the pressure on the others.

The game had started and Liverpool were attacking. There was a moment of excitement as the ball hit the bar at the far end of the pitch and Liverpool almost scored. The crowd surged forward in anticipation and the crush intensified.

Bruce Grobbelaar, who was in the Liverpool goal, could see the problem and people in the crowd shouted to him in panic.

"Bruce, they're killing us. You've got to get them to open the gate."

Bruce spoke to a policeman who didn't want to know.

"I haven't got a key. The stewards have got them. I can't do anything."

On the terrace, Ed seemed to move forward with the crowd. He found himself pressed up against the fence, with a vast weight pushing him from behind. He felt his body caving in, as if all the breath was being squeezed out. His hands tried to shield his face and push back away from the wire, but it was hopeless. All around him people were fighting for their lives, struggling for every painful breath.

The police lined up along the touchline facing the terrace and watched as a terrible scene unfolded in front of their eyes. People wondered afterwards why it took them so long to open the gate to save the dying. They stood on guard, fearing a pitch invasion should the fence give way but the fence had been constructed to contain and so it did: the living and the dead. The police were obeying orders and some were themselves traumatised by what they saw.

When the realisation finally dawned and the gate was opened, the crowd flooded onto the pitch. For many, it was too late.

Ed gasped, feeling a crushing weight on his chest. He struggled for air and felt darkness closing in around him. He was fighting for every breath but it was getting harder. The black descended on him and he lost consciousness. Don and Terry had steered him towards the gate and out onto the pitch. Out in the open, Ed became aware of the drama that was being played out around him. He felt better and seemed to look down onto the grass at frantic activity.

Don lay on the grass gasping but Terry had pulled down a hoarding with a fellow red and rushed towards one of the bodies lying on the ground. As they lifted the person carefully, something fell out of his pocket; it was a birthday card. Don saw the white envelope out of the corner of his eye and forced himself off the ground to retrieve it. They had to post it, Ed had said so. He put it in his own pocket, wiping a tear away with his other hand.

Good old, Don. He'll post the card, but what a birthday for our kid. I've gone and ruined it! The card had confirmed what Ed already knew; he was dead. It was his body on the make-shift stretcher and it was too late to save him.

A ball should have moved around the pitch, thrilling the spectators in the excitement of an FA Cup semi-final, with passion and concentration centred on twenty-two players. Instead, fans raced up and down the pitch, ferrying the dead and dying on makeshift stretchers made from advertising hoardings, in a desperate attempt to save lives. Ed, now an observer, marvelled at the heroism of the supporters, battling against all odds. He was horrified to see the police, many almost frozen in shock. They looked around for orders and didn't seem to be receiving any that they were able to follow. Some of them clearly realised that they were at fault. They should have opened the gate to allow supporters on to the pitch, instead of being determined to stop them. They could have saved many of the people who lay dead and dying : victims of prejudice and poor decision making. They were useless and yet they were supposed to be there to keep people safe. These were innocent people who only wanted to see a football match: football, England's national sport.

Ed went over to the place where Don was still lying, recovering.

"Hey mate. You're going to be all right. Thanks for trying to to help me. I'm OK. It's not the end. I don't know what happens next or if they play football in Heaven. I guess I'm going to find out."

Of course, Don couldn't hear him but he sensed others who could. The private pain gradually joined to form a cloud of intense emotion. It was like a fog which made the scene unreal. A combination of the harsh reality of the fight to save the innocent lives of football fans and the confusion of those who found they had survived death.

At one end of the pitch, a lone ambulance had finally arrived; this was not an efficient demonstration of emergency procedure. What had gone wrong?

Ed was aware of so many colours in the mist around him. The pink and purple of love, mixed with the grey and black darkness of grief and despair. His thoughts were pulled back to Carol at home in Southport and he could sense her feelings as she stood powerless in front of the television screen with scenes of horror unfolding before her eyes. How he wanted to tell her that he loved her; he would always love her. The thoughts made him feel warm and pulled him towards a bright light but it was mixed with so much pain and gradually anger was creeping in with a dark intensity.

Why? Why had all this happened to him, to all these supporters who just wanted a day out cheering on their team? He felt the sense of guilt which consumed the police, but knew that the enormity of the tragedy had sent them into denial. They had herded supporters into Leppings Lane and caused the crush that followed. Other parts of the ground were less than full but they continued to send fans to their death. Ed could hear the excuses of those in charge that day, those who were supposed to keep the fans safe. Their voices rang in his head; they clamoured for attention, bombarding his soul with their own self pity. He pushed their feelings away with anger and disgust. They would never lift the shame of that day, no matter how hard they tried, of that he was sure.

Ed could see other souls wandering around. They were confused and distraught, having difficulty coming to terms with their situation. Many were isolated by their own emotions, realising that they could not communicate with the living (whose angry tears tore at their heart strings), nor could they influence events. Colours swirled above the pitch, reflecting pain, anger, love and sadness: black, red, pink, purple and blue, like a mist enclosing their souls. Gradually, they were drawn to each other; the older ones comforting the younger and holding out hands to guide them through the trauma of death. It was hard to pull away from the scene of drama and despair. Heroic supporters were fighting to save lives, while those in charge panicked and sought to avoid blame. These mixed emotions pulled at the souls to remain earthbound.

Anger made Ed feel cold and started to pull him down into darkness. His soul was racked with tremors of agony, even though he was no longer able to feel physical pain. Somehow, a voice crept through his desolation; a lone voice, singing words he knew so well.

'When you walk through a storm, hold your head up high.'

He listened intently and felt that same emotion of camaraderie he always felt when he heard the song.

'And don't be afraid of the dark.'

Through the mist of emotions, he could see the figure still holding a red scarf. He moved towards the sound.

'At the end of the storm, there's a golden sky.'

Others were also drawn in, joining with their voices.

'And the sweet silver song of a lark.'

Outstretched hands linked together and around them, a light, pink, purple, white and then golden could be seen. Strong and powerful, it was the only way to go.

'Walk on through the wind, walk on through the rain, though your dreams be tossed and blown.'

Never had these words been so true. Dreams of a team's glory and dreams of life had burnt so bright at the start of that April day.

'Walk on, walk on, with hope in your heart and you'll never walk alone.'

The singing drew the souls together and they reached out to one another with a bond of allegiance. It was a clarion call they all recognised so that the lost and confused were gathered into the group with love and protection. Rising above the drama still being played out on the pitch, they walked as one, into the bright, golden light.

'You'll never walk alone.'

Justice for the 96 supporters who lost their lives at Hillsborough on 15th April 1989. Always remembered.

On Wednesday 20th April 2016, the jury at the inquests gave a verdict of Unlawful Killing of the 96 Liverpool Supporters who died at Hillsborough. They had taken two years to reach this verdict but the dead, the families and the survivors finally achieved justice.

THE TERRORIST

He approached the busy railway station with determination. The passing faces of travellers drew no emotion from him. He did not observe the mothers with young children, excited, anticipating a day filled with wonder in the capital city, or the babies crying at the beginning of their life's journey. Old couples, their closeness moulded by the years, were smiling with contentment as they enjoyed a rare venture into the fast-paced city life. Young people were rushing, with no time to lose, so many places to go, so many things to do. None of these registered in the mind of the young man filled with hate and the ambition to become a martyr: at least to those of his own religion.

He moved carefully, only too aware of the precious cargo he carried. He was used to the weight after so many hours of practice. A dummy run weeks ago had shown him how to carry the load without drawing too much attention to himself or causing a premature accident. His mission should be accomplished as planned, nothing would be allowed to go wrong. Everything was rehearsed, down to the last second. All would proceed according to plan.

He walked up to the newspaper stand and bought a paper. Pausing, he glanced at the headlines with derision. How ironic, tomorrow, he would be the headline. He laughed but looked around furtively. Did he detect a tremor? Was he starting to panic? Nothing must stop the plan. They had all worked too long for it to fail; he must not let them down. He must be careful, arrogance could give everything away; there were those who watched for people like him. Still he gloated, silently. His name would be on everyone's lips in the morning. The world would know how much he had lived and died for the cause. Would they understand that they had to pay; that his kind would win in the end? At least that was what he believed, what he had to believe.

He found a vacant seat among the tired travellers. Again, he resisted the temptation to look at them. They were not important; numbers caught up in a moment of history. He looked at his watch, closed his eyes uttering a silent prayer and shouted, *'Allahu akbar,'* which means 'God is greatest' in Arabic. He then pulled the cord clasped between his fingers.

At three minutes past one, Waterloo Station exploded with a bang and flash of blinding light. Dust and debris rained down, screams rent the air and the living rushed in panic as far and as fast as they could from the devastation. Sirens could be heard all around London as the emergency services responded to the call they had dreaded but prepared for. When the immediate chaos had subsided, many ran to help using makeshift stretchers to carry the injured, stemming blood with random items of clothing and comforting the walking wounded with whatever kind words they could utter.

He was there, suspended above the turmoil, though untouched: an observer. His head reeled in confusion. Where was Paradise? Where was his honoured welcome? It would come, of course; he must have to wait. Perhaps he had to witness the carnage, the result of his endeavours. He looked around, aware of everything happening at the station. The bloody body parts scattered far and wide belonged to him and others. He recognised his own flesh amid the pieces of charred clothing and knowing he had survived, felt a shock shuddering through his now complete body. As he thought about what he had done, his whole being was pulled down towards the blood and burning. He saw police and ambulance men racing towards the scene of his crime. He heard a commotion behind him.

"It's him! That's the murderer! Come on, let's get the swine who did this!" The menacing faces of his victims closed in on him. Fists raised in anger, they attacked him to no avail. He was dead and could not be hurt in a physical way. Realising that they could not take revenge, the victims were devastated, consumed with anger and frustration. Their powerful emotions sent shock waves around the scene which was already reeling with the aftermath of tragedy. The feeling bore down upon the bomber not like a wave, but a tsunami. His mind connected with the dead who surrounded him and he experienced the trauma and pain of every one of them. Darkness engulfed him and his soul cried out in torment. He struggled to find a way out of his prison, but he was caught in the grip of unrelenting despair.

He tried to speak to them, to explain, but the words would not come. All the rhetoric dissolved into nothing. His mind was numb. They turned from him, knowing that his mental suffering would be greater than any physical wound they could inflict. For a moment, he felt a pang of sorrow, and wondered why he had committed such an act. His feelings sparked an awareness of a light that some of those around him were being drawn towards. Near the light, he saw an angelic being radiating brightness. Waves of blue and green light emanated from the being, flooding the scene almost like a comforting blanket. More and more people were being pulled towards the angel, though not all. He tried to join the stream of dead moving towards the light, but he felt a dark barrier in front of him.

A booming voice called out. "Stop! Not you!"

"Why not? I'm going to Paradise! I was promised. I've been preparing myself for this."

A cruel laugh echoed around him.

"Paradise! They won't have you. They don't have murderers. We have them, ha, ha. Come with us where it's nice and dark. You can even try to forget…if we let you…but then we won't, ha, ha, ha. I love these chances to collect a few more. Not as if we're running out though. Our numbers keep growing! There's no Paradise for you: no virgins, not even one, ha, ha, ha!"

"But I was told…"

Suddenly the things he had been told seemed like shallow lies. However, in desperation, he tried again.

"I did it for God." He felt a hard lump in his throat as he choked the words out. The laughter became manic.

"This gets better, you're a great one! You've been listening to fools. God won't have anyone who kills his children. That's what they'd tell you, if they bothered to notice you. What happens is, we get you. But then we're all like you in one way or another. All suffering for what we did on Earth."

The bomber stared hard at his victims who were being guided towards the light. He was overwhelmed with self loathing and turned away, knowing that he could not bear to look. He peered into the darkness but could not see the owner of the voice although it had been so clear. The knowledge of his fate was becoming clearer and he was beginning to wonder what lay in store for him. He was flooded with self pity. Why had this happened to him? He thought of the people who had encouraged him, who had pushed him into this, persuading and training him. Why couldn't they do it themselves if they wanted it so much? They had set him up for their own ends and now he was the one to suffer, dammed for all eternity. His anger pulled him strongly into the darkness and he knew there was no escape.

His mind raced. It was not his fault, it was their fault. He could explain, he could! The alternative was too dreadful even to think about. Desperately, he forced himself to move towards the light. His body felt like lead and the pull from the darkness was overwhelming.

The voice thundered out, breaking through the heavy silence.

"You are a murderer! You are wasting time looking for excuses. The light would hurt you. Keep away from it. You have brought pain and misery to God's world. There is no hope for you. You must feel it. You have a dark soul, full of hate. You can't stand the light, it will burn you up."

He looked back and winced as the rays of light pierced him with pain. He cried out in surprise and turned away quickly. He drifted into a thick mist ahead. It was a fog of emotion. All he could hear was uncontrollable crying. The distraught sobs and cries of the bereaved flooded over him but he was deaf to their anguish, feeling only self-pity because he was being dragged down to Hell by his despicable act. High above, through the darkness, he caught sight of angelic wings surrounded by radiant light. The angels were sending comfort, but fiery voices warned him once again, shouting and screeching.

"It hurts, it hurts! Don't look at it. You are dammed like us. There's no salvation for you. It's too late, too late!"

Despite the warning, he forced himself to look into the light and heard another voice, lighter and more melodic this time.

"Feel the pain of your victims and their loved ones; understand their feelings. Ask for their forgiveness and accept that you have wronged them. Pray to God for his mercy and help. Turn away from your evil intent and begin your journey of healing. Renounce violence. The universe is founded on love; there is no place for hatred."

He was suspended in a whirlwind of pain and emotion, pulled one way and then another. Had he been wrong? Had he committed a foul act against humanity? Could he take the suffering and start to put things right. Would he ever be granted forgiveness? Was he capable of wiping the slate clean even though it would be a long, hard road of atonement?

The voices of damnation laughed and gloated.

"He is evil. He was always ours!"

Despite the pull of gloom, the angels were still there, shining their healing rays, blue, green, purple and the brightest white light he had ever seen. This must indeed be Paradise, but it was not for him; it was for the innocent dead and they streamed into it, now surrounded with the pink light of love.

The spark of God within him cried out as it felt their pain and anguish. They were leaving loved ones behind who did not even know that they were gone and it rent their souls. He began to feel the emotion that he had tried so hard to block out, but strangely, he felt better for having suffered it. Almost at once he recognised that he had begun his own journey of salvation. A small ripple of warmth crossed his shade, soothing the depths of his being. All was not lost, he knew that now. The demons of darkness could not believe they were losing him. They renewed their attack.

"Pain, pain, that is all you will get. It will burn you up. That light is too bright for your dark soul. You are ours; you must hide as we do."

They had to be right, he thought, turning back once again. This time a shadow of doubt crossed his shade. The warmth wasn't like burning, it was lacking in anger, yet, there was a sadness that tore at his very soul, so that he could have shed buckets of tears, had he a physical body. He knew he had felt God's pain that one of his children could inflict such harm. As he moved closer to the light, he understood completely. The universe was indeed built upon love and he had committed an unnatural act. He was suffused with pity but this time the pity was for his victims and their families; there was none for himself. He couldn't believe how wrong he had been. His ghost trembled with self-loathing and despair. He had murdered in God's name: the ultimate blasphemy.

He spun round sharply. His soul shouted out, torn with self-disgust, as he realised that he had lived and died a lie.

"Let me rot in Hell. It's all I deserve. How could I break the laws of God and of humanity? I am so sorry. I have sinned in the most despicable way."

Even as the words came, he sensed that this true and deeply felt acknowledgement was part of his own healing. The warmth around him grew but its compassion still served to emphasise his crime against humankind. The evil voices which had been so loud were becoming dim, although they were loath to give up. He shrank away into the dark, overwhelmed by his unworthiness but then forced himself to move a little closer to the light.

Suffused with sadness, he felt God's love and forgiveness start to fire the spark within his heart. He knew that there would be a long journey with much to accomplish before he could make amends, but also, that there was hope. Perhaps he could enter God's Kingdom knowing that he had already begun to learn?

In so many ways, he would have to start again. Whatever was demanded of him he would do. He was deeply aware of the pain he had inflicted upon the innocents who he had not even been prepared to notice. Deep within the horror of what he had done, he would have to find a way to heal others; a way to prevent those like him from committing this sin against humanity. This he felt would be his mission and his road towards healing. With this knowledge flooding through his being, he moved forward and slowly, he began to merge with the light.

THE STONE SEAT

Sculpted stone stands forgotten, carved vines, ivy covered.
Resting amid nettles, bramble scratched, twisting heavenward.
Abandoned now, this garden of melancholy.
Silent in moonlit nights and sun drenched days.
Shade shadowed, the moss clings, covering stone secrets,
Safe, silent and undisturbed.

Approaching, slow footsteps along the well worn path.
Gnarled hands clear aged growth, carefully pulling leaves away.
Smooth stone revealed, space cleared, to rest amid fond memories.
His life's evening, dappled sunlight, through dipped willow branches.
In dozing comfort, his fingers travel, finding images, stone suspended.
Eyes closing, he drifts into the recess of his mind and rolls back years.

Here, one hot July, love bloomed, intoxicating, with rose petal scent,
Red as blood on sun bleached stone, whispered promises, a stolen kiss.
War brought parting, his letters penned through years of sadness.
Tear washed stone, prayers, eyes read ink- blurred words.

Hope rewarded, faith redeemed, reunited; time began once more.
Soft evenings breathed new life into the stone.

Quiet companionship, stone solid through the years,
Amid life's changing history, created refuge from its storms.
Surrounded by still, summer days of contentment, tea and cakes.
Perfumed flowers pressed between the pages of her books.
Solitude of reading, or delight as laughter echoed round the stone.
Children's games, stories told, gifts of wisdom and exchange of news.

One day, returned from church, dazed, numbed by grief,
White lilies lay on the saddened stone. He sought her comfort.
Drinking in the past, where love remained, despite its emptiness.
Lonely thoughts of long gone days, lost forever in the sands of time.
He sat, stone statue-like, gaze suspended, deep in reverie. Motionless,
As if the plants would claim him, part of the garden and the past.

Weed-choked stone, neglected monument, joys and life forgotten.
As in tired sorrow, years passed by with housebound illness.
Now, though weak, he rests his body on the warm, strong seat.

Familiar voices drifting on the gentle breeze re-ignite the past.

Eyes closed, the sunset of his days, with hands caressing stone,

He sighs in readiness, smiles and gently breathes his last.

ILLUSTRATIONS

1. St. Mary the Virgin Church, St. Mary in the Marsh, Kent, England, showing the grave of writer Edith Nesbit.
2. Hospital room.
3. Anubis the god of the Underworld and the Scales of Ma'at.
4. Statue of Jesus Christ in St. Vitus Cathedral, Prague, Czech Republic.
5. An arrow marker on the battlefield of the Battle of Hastings (14th October 1066) at Battle Abbey, East Sussex, England.
6. Fresco of the murder of Thomas Becket in St. Augustine Church, Brookland, Kent. England. Thomas Becket murdered 29th December, 1170.
7. Interior of St. Clement Church, Old Romney, Kent. England.
8. North American Indian.
9. Minuteman Statue at Battle Green, Lexington, Massachusetts, USA. Battle of Lexington and Concord, 19[Th] April, 1775.
10. Cowboy.
11. Anglo-Boer War Memorial. Museum of Military History, Saxonwold, Johannesburg, South Africa. In memory of the soldiers who served and died in the 1899-1902, Anglo-Boer War.
12. Chilston Park Hotel staircase. Lenham, Kent, England.

13. Old horseracing.

14. Gangster.

15. The Battle of Britain Memorial, Capel- le -Ferne, Kent. Battle of Britain (10th July, 1940 to 31st October, 1940).

16. Statue 'Il Commendatore' in memory of W.A Mozart's Don Giovanni by Anna Chromy, Prague. Czech Republic.

17. Tunnel with graffiti.

18. Liverpool FC flag on the Kop at Anfield, Liverpool, England.

19. Commuters.

20. Painshill, Cobham, Surrey, England.

Printed in the United States
By Bookmasters